SKETCHING
UNDERCOVER

SKETCHING UNDERCOVER

First edition. April 2022.

Cover design by 100 Covers

Editor: Brooke De Lira

ISBN: 979-8-9855366-1-4

SKETCHING UNDERCOVER

T.K. Price

DEDICATION

I'd like to thank my wonderful family for always believing in
me and letting me chase my dreams. I love you all.

Chapter 1

Art. It was my passion. I had wanted to draw, paint, color, and everything in between since I could hold a pencil or paintbrush. My parents had encouraged it. Until I decided to get my degree in fine arts. They weren't too excited about that. For four years, they tried to steer me into another degree. One that held more weight and got me a "real job"— whatever that is. But I persevered and graduated with honors at my fine arts school.

Here was the hitch. Six years after graduating, I had been bouncing from one random project to another, and things weren't going well. Honestly, I was starting to regret my decision. People always say you should choose a job you'll love doing. Even though I did just that, I was still left trying to scrounge up enough money to pay my landlord and keep my lights on. During my college years, I had no idea it would be this rough to unite my passion for art with a steady income.

"Oh my God. This is awful," my current client, Patrice Martel, squealed.

I looked down at my paintbrush, seeing that the sky-blue paint had dripped onto the dark-walnut table beneath me. I had placed a tarp over it earlier, but my client's dastardly dog, Chico the Chow Chow, must have messed with it while I was zoned out. I clambered down from the step stool and surveyed the antique table that was now splattered with blue paint. I looked sheepishly over at the woman, who was decked out in a fancy dress and cashmere scarf.

Her light-blue eyes narrowed on me. "Do you know how much this cost?"

"I'm guessing you didn't get it from IKEA, so probably a lot," I answered with a nervous chuckle.

"Five thousand dollars. Now it's worthless because of you."

"Well, if you would have locked up that mangy mutt like I asked," I said, pointing toward the dog lounging by his bowl, "this wouldn't have happened."

Her mouth dropped in shock as she threw a delicate hand over her chest. "How dare you accuse me and my darling Chico. All you millennials and Gen-Zers are the same. Can't take responsibility for your own actions."

"Listen, lady, I'm not going to fight with you. I know when I make a mistake, and this isn't one of them."

"You're fired. Take your things and go. Your services are no longer needed."

"Great. I didn't like working here anyway," I snapped.

She huffed before turning away, stomping toward her kitchen. Halfway there, she called over her shoulder, "And I hope you're aware this will be docked from your final paycheck."

"Gee, I would have never guessed," I muttered under my breath.

Sucking in a deep breath, I cleaned up what I could before packing my stuff to leave. I pulled my black messenger bag across my torso, letting it rest on my left shoulder. Heading to the foyer, I noticed a check with my name on it lying on the table near the front entrance. Even though Patrice had said she was going to pay me, I was still surprised. I checked the balance. More than half of my earnings had been deducted. She usually paid me around five hundred dollars for the work. Today, I was left with a measly one hundred bucks.

I scoffed, shoving my crappy payment into my bag before exiting the luxury mansion. It was a bright and sweltering summer day in South Florida. I could already feel my body starting to sweat as I made my way to my scooter. Placing my black helmet on my head, I took off toward my run-down apartment. It was a quick ride since most people were still at work, which translated to lighter traffic. When I stepped through my doorway, I found my roommate, Natalie, passed out on the couch. Her left arm and adjacent leg were hanging off, her head pressed up against the armrest. Part of her wavy auburn-colored hair fanned around her face while the rest was up in the loose bun she wore. I kicked her foot lightly, making her stir, but her snoring continued to flood the room. I kicked her a second time, and her olive-green eyes fluttered open.

She craned her neck back to look at me and groaned, "What are you doing home?"

"I could ask you the same thing." I tossed my stuff onto our messy loveseat.

"I took off today. . . I had a long night."

"I'm sure you did. What was his name? Ron? Sean?"

"His name was Léon."

"Right. Thanks for ditching me, by the way," I grumbled.

She sat up, stretching her long limbs with a yawn. "He was hot, and sweet too. And did you hear his accent? So sexy."

"He was all right. But you think almost every man you meet is sexy."

"That's not true. There have been a few exceptions. Anyway, why are you home?"

I plopped down next to her and sighed, running a hand through my short-cropped black curls. "I was fired."

"Welp, I'm not surprised. That lady was a pain in the a—"

"Natalie! She was not that bad."

"Not that bad? The day I helped you paint, she was walking all over you like a worn-out carpet."

I nodded reluctantly. "I admit she was kind of annoying, but she paid well and kept me employed for way longer than I'd expected."

"That's true. I want to say she only kept you around because she felt sorry for you, but I doubt she has any feelings."

I rolled my eyes and flopped backward, sinking further into our frayed couch. I rubbed four fingers against my temple and asked, "What am I going to do? Your job won't be enough to pay our rent."

Natalie rested her chin on her fist. "My paycheck will barely cover our utilities."

"We already had to cut the cable. I guess the internet is next."

She gasped at the unspeakable thought. "Whoa, I don't think we need to jump that far ahead. You just got fired. Plus, you still have some money in your savings account."

"How do you know?" I gave her a side-eye, raising an

eyebrow.

Natalie shrugged, a small, cheeky smirk on her lips. "I know you. You're always thinking ahead, and you're smart with your finances. We should last a couple of months until you find another project."

"I guess you're right. The thing is, I have no idea what I'm going to do. I haven't seen anything in our area that would call for my art degree."

"I heard the local elementary school is looking for an art teacher."

I sneered in disgust and said, "That's not where I was planning on working when I got my degree."

"At least it's something."

"I'll keep it in mind. For now, I'm just going to scour job sites and see what else pops up."

"That's the spirit." Natalie bounced up from the couch and grabbed her purse off the kitchen counter. She dug into the large bag, pulling out a twenty. "I knew I had some money left over. Why don't we party it up tonight? It'll make you feel better."

I glanced over at her and mumbled, "I don't think so. And you can't miss work tomorrow."

"I'm not going home with anyone tonight. Just a few drinks, you and me."

"Only if we go to Tino's."

"Why Tino's?"

"Because pretty much everyone there is married and over twice our age."

Natalie nodded in approval. "That's true. They have good pizza too."

"Yes. Two birds, one stone," I said with a grin.

We decided to change into some casual dress clothes before heading out to our local bar and grill.

We didn't make it home until one in the morning, but I wasn't tired enough to head straight to bed. Since I didn't need to be up early for work, I wound up surfing the net for jobs in the area. I stumbled on the teacher position Natalie had mentioned. It offered decent pay, but I wasn't classroom material. It's not that I hated kids. But working with them for five days a week, five hours a day wasn't on my to-do list. I scrolled through half the pages on the job-search website. The available positions in my field ranged from cartoonist to art critic. I didn't seem to qualify for any of them since I had no experience in those specific fields, but I jotted them down anyway. I fell asleep at my computer desk, waking up around noon when a knock sounded at the front door.

I trudged over to the door, not even bothering to look through the peephole as I swung it open. My brother, older than me by a mere four years, was standing there in a gray suit and black dress shirt. His black hair was cut short with a temple fade, and a small hint of a goatee was forming on his walnut skin. He wore a mischievous grin and his medium brown eyes glistened as he said, "You look like crap, Cal."

"Thanks, Bryan. It's nice to see you too," I grumbled.

"Mom wanted me to check on you."

"She could have called."

"She didn't think you'd answer, especially after the last phone call."

I rolled my eyes as I recalled our last chat over the phone.

She'd been nagging me on my job choices, hoping I'd finally get something steady instead of jumping from gig to gig. I wanted her to be proud of me, but I always felt like I wasn't good enough. My brother was the golden child. But me? I was the black sheep.

I crossed my arms and snapped, "Well, if she'd let me do what I love instead of belittling every choice I've made, maybe I would talk to her more often."

"She doesn't do that," he replied.

"Maybe not to you. She's happy for you. And she takes every chance to express that too. 'Why couldn't you get a normal job like your brother? Why couldn't you be valedictorian like your brother? Why aren't you, just in general, more like your brother?'"

He gave me a sympathetic smile. "She's only looking out for you, Cal. Mom and Dad love you, but they want to see you succeed. I want to see that too, because I know you can."

"I just wish she'd dial it down a bit," I said, staring at the floor.

"I'll talk with her."

"No, I don't need you butting in," I said, a cutting-edge seeping into my voice.

He shrugged with a huff. "Fine, I'll let you two handle it."

"So, is that all? Because I'm kind of busy."

"Doing what? Sleeping?"

"I was up late last night, okay?"

"Why?"

"Finding a job. . ." I mumbled just loud enough for him to hear.

"You lost your job?" he yelled, throwing his hands up dramatically.

"It wasn't my intention, but the woman was a prude."

He scoffed, placing both hands on his hips. "Callie, that was decent money you were making with her. How are you going to pay the rent?"

"You don't think I haven't thought of that? I'll figure something out. I usually do."

"Listen, I know you'd rather do your own thing, or even get into a gallery. But maybe you should look for something permanent this time. You're twenty-eight; you need to think about a sustainable income."

"I'm aware of that, and I'm thinking about it. I came across a few job openings I found, but I don't know if they're right for me."

"If you're interested, I might be able to get you an interview. I know it's not your cup of tea, but it's a job."

I peered at my brother with my head tilted and my eyebrows scrunched. "What is it?"

"The Miami-Dade Police Department is looking for a sketch artist to work part-time. We usually pick from a pool of specialized artists to work a case, or we get someone who's already in law enforcement. Lately, they've been thinking about creating a permanent position. They want someone to be at the ready as soon as we have a case," he answered.

"I don't know. It's not even full-time."

"The salary is pretty solid though, and I think they're throwing in benefits as well. It couldn't hurt to give it a shot."

"Don't I need special training for that?"

"You do, but they'll provide classes to get you up to speed on the skills you'll need for the job."

My shoulders sagged as I let out a short hum. "It could be interesting. It's not like I have many choices anyway."

"True, and if you get the training from us, you'll be able to work at any department for some cash. Being a freelance sketch artist isn't the best gig when you're not on the force itself, but it's a starting point."

I sucked in a breath, feeling a spark of determination. "I'll take the interview."

Bryan smiled as he pulled me into a bone-crushing hug. He kissed the top of my head and said, "I'm proud of you, Callie. Plus, if you get the job, we'll be seeing a lot more of each other."

"You know, on second thought, I take it back. I don't want the job," I joked as I tried to wiggle out of his grasp.

"Nope, it's too late. I'm talking to my captain and the HR manager today to see if we can squeeze you in."

"All right. . . Now let me go."

He unfurled his arms from around me, and I took in a large breath of air before releasing my breath slowly. My brother gave me a wide, crooked grin and said, "I'll text you if I hear anything, okay?"

"That's fine," I replied as he started for the door. "And Bryan, thanks."

He turned back to shoot me one last smile. "Anything for my baby sister."

He exited my apartment, and I locked the door behind him. I wasn't sure if working for the police was what I wanted to do with my life. Still, it would be fun to help solve crimes with my art. Since I had nothing but time on my hands, I figured I should look up more information on what sketch artists do while I waited for my brother's call.

Chapter 2

I spent the next two days scouring information on forensic sketch artists. It seemed like I was in for a lot of training if I wound up getting the job. Necessary skills ranged from composite art and imaging to age progression and even facial recognition. The total amount of training was said to be forty hours and would last for about a week, depending on what program the MDPD set me up for. The only subject I wasn't looking forward to was science. It had never been my strong suit back in school, and I doubted that had changed. I just hoped I could pull it off to nab the job.

I was sat at the table drinking a freshly brewed cup of coffee. It was still piping hot, so I took my time sipping the sweet breakfast blend with peppermint mocha creamer. The rejuvenating beverage was exactly what I needed to kick-start my day. As I flipped through the unpaid bills on the breakfast nook, Natalie walked out dressed in her waitress outfit.

"You have the morning shift today?" I asked.

She nodded as she helped herself to a cup of the coffee I had just made. As she stirred in her sugar and creamer, she answered, "I decided to take a couple more shifts at the restaurant since you got fired."

"You didn't have to do that."

"I know, but I haven't pulled my weight much since I started living here. So, I figured I'd do my part."

"Thanks, Nat. I hope I can get back on my feet soon."

Natalie sat next to me at our compact nook. Taking a sip of her coffee, she asked, "How is the job search coming along?"

I toyed with the tiny curls at the nape of my neck, letting out a drawn-out sigh. "It could be better. I'm still waiting on my brother to call me about that sketch-artist gig."

"Do you think you'll be a good fit there?"

"Not a clue, but it's worth a shot. I mean, it is still in my wheelhouse. I'll be doing what I love, even though it'll be more complicated and draining."

"Can you even handle that kind of stress? You're going to be listening to a lot of people's trauma stories and seeing some gruesome things."

I nursed my coffee, imagining what it would be like to sketch a dangerous criminal. "I know it's going to be rough, but I'm willing to try it. At least for a little while."

Natalie patted my back as she got up. "I'm rooting for you, Callie. I think you'll do a great job if you get it."

I followed her into the kitchen, and we placed our empty cups into the sink. "I hope so, because this is kind of my last resort. Otherwise, I'll be teaching elementary school students how to draw stick figures and mold clay for the rest of my life."

"Don't be so pessimistic. I'm sure you'd be teaching the kids more than that."

I shook my head with a chuckle. "I'm sure the curriculum would be a little more tedious. It's still not what I had in mind when I got my degree."

"Understandable." Natalie strode to the door, grabbing her keys and purse off of the side table. "I should get going before Eduardo chews me out again. What do you have planned today?"

"Not much. I'll probably go grocery shopping since we need some food, and then do more job searching."

"Ooh, can you grab some little cinnamon donut holes? I love those."

"I was only planning on grabbing the essentials given our financial situation."

Her shoulders slumped as she gave me a pout. "Aw, fine. Maybe I'll get some good tips today, and I can put it toward our future grocery splurge."

"Sounds good to me." I waved her off as she opened the door to leave. "Have a good time at work."

I decided to get the grocery shopping out of the way, so I could focus on my job search for the rest of the day. After jotting down a quick list on a scrap of paper that I found in our kitchen junk drawer, I headed off to the store.

Grocery shopping wound up taking longer than I had anticipated. It's not like I had anywhere to be. I just didn't want to spend my downtime roaming around half-stocked aisles and avoiding older shoppers who were shuffling slowly behind their carts. After arriving home and putting the groceries away, I went to my room to start the job search once again. Before I could even open my laptop, my phone rang.

I checked the caller ID and groaned at the name displayed on the screen. It was my mother. I had no interest in answering, but avoiding her would do me no good. Sucking up what little pride I had, I picked up the call. "Hi, Mom. What's up?"

"I heard you lost your job," she said in a serious tone.

"So, we're jumping right in, huh?"

"Callie, you haven't had a steady job since you got out of college. You need to take a hard look at your life and figure out what you want to do."

I flopped back onto my bed. My feet were dangling off the floor as I stared up at the chipped and discolored ceiling above. "I *do* know what I want to do. I want to draw and create art. It's the only thing I'm passionate about."

"You could always do it on the side as a hobby. But it's no profession, dear. You need to think about your future."

"I am thinking about my future. Every day I think about it. But I know working a boring nine-to-five job will never make me happy, and I want to do something that does."

She sighed. "Sometimes, it's not about happiness. It's about practicality. I worked as a realtor for thirty-seven years, and it sure didn't make me happy, at least not every day. But it paid the bills and got both of my children through college."

I peeked over at the cluttered art desk in the far corner of my room. "I know that. I'll figure it out, though. You don't have to worry."

"You're a smart girl, Callie. I just don't want to see you throwing your life away for a pipe dream."

Silence stretched between us for a brief moment as I took

in her words. After ten years of fighting for the life and career I wanted, I was starting to believe that my parents were right. Maybe I wasn't cut out to be an artist, at least not in the way I'd hoped. As I sat up, a tear fell from my eye. I quickly wiped it away and tried to escape the conversation. "I have to go, Mom. I'll talk to you later."

My mother rushed out her sentence as she tried to keep me on the line. "We're having a family dinner tonight at seven. Will you be able to make it?"

I lowered my head and whispered, "I'll see if I can."

Without letting her say another word, I hung up and tossed my phone aside. I got off the bed and made my way over to the black art table. Dozens of half-finished pieces of artwork were scattered around the small space along with pencils and ink pens. Hot tears rolled down my cheeks, and my nose flared as I stared down at the pieces. Lifting my right arm, I raked it across the desk and watched as the papers, pencils, and pens flew onto the carpeted ground. The artwork that remained intact on the table, I snatched and started ripping it to pieces.

When I finished decimating my art, I slid down the wall and gazed over the mess I'd made. My chest was heaving uncontrollably as I tried to catch my breath and slow my crying. Feeling drained, both mentally and physically, I crawled over to my bed. I climbed under my unmade covers, pulling the rumpled sheets up and over my head. Lying in the makeshift darkness I'd created, I drifted off to sleep thinking about my uncertain future.

My eyes fluttered open when I felt my bed shake violently. I jolted up, the covers that had enveloped my face falling into my lap in the process. Searching for the culprit, I looked to the foot of my bed to see Natalie laughing hysterically with her arm over her stomach. I groaned as she continued to laugh at my expense. "What are you doing?"

"Your door was open, and I saw you were sleeping. Thought I'd scare you a bit," she said with a few more giggles escaping her lips.

"Not cool."

She shrugged as she sat on the edge of my bed, scanning the floor of my room. "What happened in here? Did a tornado blow through?"

"I had a little discussion with my mother about my art. I got frustrated and took it out on my work."

"She still doesn't care about your life choices, huh?"

"Nope. And honestly, I'm starting to believe she's right."

"She's not." Natalie picked up one of my sketches that was still intact. She held it up for both of us to see. "This is amazing, and it isn't even complete. I'd give anything to draw more than some lopsided shapes and a stick figure."

I wriggled over to her and snatched the paper from her hand. "Do you even know what it is?"

"It's a zombie."

"It's my great-grandmother before she died.'

"That was my second guess." Natalie wrapped her skinny arm around my shoulders and pulled me toward her. "Don't fret over this. Just because you've had a rough year or two, doesn't mean you should give up on your dream. You'll strike gold eventually. It's just not your time yet."

I locked my eyes on the unfinished picture of my great-grandmother and said, "You're right, Nat. A few bumps in the road are normal for anyone. One day my degree will pay off, but for now, I'll focus on another career. Until my hobby takes me to where I want to be."

"That's the spirit." Natalie glanced at the watch on her wrist and grumbled, "What's for supper tonight? I'm starving."

"What time is it?"

"A quarter to seven."

I leaped off the bed and flew to my dresser in the middle of my room. As I pulled out clothes to wear, Natalie asked, "Where are you heading?"

"I have dinner with my parents and my brother at seven. We're already on bad terms. I don't need to add being late to the record."

"Aw, so we're not going out tonight?"

"Afraid not."

"I guess I'll order takeout."

When I reached the doorway of my room, I turned back to Natalie and said, "Thanks for the chat. I needed it."

She gave me a wide grin. "Any time. I don't want to see my friend moping around for something she should be proud of."

I gave her a brief nod before scurrying to the bathroom to get ready for an exhausting family dinner.

Ten minutes after seven, I pulled into the driveway of my parents' extravagant home on the other side of town. Bryan's black Lexus was parked next to me, so I knew he was already inside. He'd probably arrived early, like always. I hopped off my scooter and placed my helmet on the right handlebar. Smoothing out my basic silk shirt and skinny jeans, I jogged up to the front door. I rang the doorbell, and it didn't take long for my mother to answer.

"You're late," she mumbled as she stepped aside for me to come in.

Lifting my shoulders innocently, I answered, "I fell asleep and lost track of time."

"Dinner just came out of the oven, so we haven't started quite yet."

I followed her into the spacious dining room where my brother and father were busy chatting. My father spotted me, and with an illuminating grin, he got up from his seat. He shuffled over to me and enveloped me in a warm bear hug. "Oh, I'm so happy you made it, snuggle bug."

I patted his thick back and said, "Hi, Dad. How're you?"

"I'm fantastic now that my baby girl is here."

"I'm not a baby anymore."

"I know, but you'll always be my baby girl, no matter what," he said as he let go of me.

My mother chimed in as she sat down in the seat next to my dad's. "Harold, can we start now before dinner gets cold?"

"Sure, Vivian. We can eat."

My dad took his seat at the dining table as I went to sit next to Bryan. He flashed me a quick grin and whispered, "I'm glad you could make it."

"I almost bailed, but I thought it was the right thing to do," I murmured back.

My mother started to dish out the food she'd prepared, which consisted of mixed vegetables, mashed potatoes, roasted chicken, and dinner rolls. Once everyone's plates were full, we started to dig in. As we enjoyed every forkful of the warm, delicious meal, my father decided to start a conversation.

"How's the detective job going for you, Son?"

"Not bad. We finally solved a case that's been eluding us for weeks, but there are still plenty more cases that are keeping our hands full," Bryan said while sipping from his wine glass.

"I'm sure there are. I remember my shifts at the hospital. Some days were good while other days, we were up to our necks with patients."

"Do you miss it? Or do you like retirement life more?"

My dad set down his fork to rub his stubbled chin in thought. "They both have their pros and cons, but retirement is quite nice. I've taken up some new hobbies and gotten to spend more time with your mother. I do miss the feeling of saving people's lives, but it was also taxing when we'd lose them."

It was my turn to be put on the spot when my mother drilled me with, "How's the job hunt going?"

"Just swell," I said, poking at a piece of broccoli with my fork.

"What are you going to do for rent?"

"I have some money saved up, and Natalie is helping out."

My mother rolled her blue-gray eyes with a huff. "Natalie. . . She barely has two nickels to rub together and is always mooching off of you. I don't know why you're still letting her live with you."

"She's my friend, and I'm sure I wouldn't find anyone remotely close to her in this day and age."

"I think Natalie is great," my father interjected, clearly trying to defuse the coming argument. "Callie is smart, and she's old enough to know how to make the right decisions."

My mother waved her right arm around as she tried to explain her thoughts. "I just don't want my daughter to wind up living on the streets because she's unemployed and her roommate is a low-life."

I scoffed. "Because you don't want your ritzy friends finding out that your daughter is a failure."

"Hey, now," my father snapped, narrowing his mahogany eyes on me. "Your mother does not think that. And you're not a failure. Right, Vivian?"

Mother stayed silent as she stared at the nearly empty plate in front of her. That was all the confirmation I needed.

"Exactly," I grumbled as I pushed my chair out and stood to leave.

Before I could get very far, Bryan grabbed my left arm and pleaded, "Can everyone drop this for a second? We're here to have a nice family dinner and spend quality time together. I'd like to have one decent meal that doesn't end in a fight."

"Just let me go, Bry," I mumbled.

"No," he barked. "Sit down, and let's complete a whole meal without someone running off."

As I sat tentatively back down in the dining chair, my mother shot my brother a hard look. "What's gotten into you, Bryan?"

"I'm tired of you two going head-to-head every time we're together. Callie may not be the next Picasso or Van Gogh, but she's trying her best, and you should support her. Quit putting her down every chance you get."

My mother sputtered as she tried to find the words to say, but it seemed like she was coming up empty. My father snickered as he drank more of his wine and said, "He's got a point."

Her shoulders sagged as she nodded in reluctant admission. She glanced up at me, actually making eye contact, something we haven't had in some time. "I'm sorry I've made you feel the way you have. I do just want what's best for you, but I'm scared you won't be able to support yourself."

I smiled meekly at her and said, "No matter what happens, I'll know how to get myself out of it. You just have to trust that I know what I'm doing."

"I do."

Bryan clapped his hands together and said, "Now that everything is settled, I have some good news to share."

"You've found a girlfriend," my mother beamed.

"No, not yet. It's actually news for Callie."

I looked over at my brother, confused. "For me?"

"Yup, it's about the sketch artist job. They would like to interview you."

My father crossed his arms over his chest. "You're thinking about getting a job with the MDPD?"

I shrugged my left shoulder. "Bryan mentioned it to me, and I thought I'd take the opportunity. I might not even get the job, though."

"Well, I think it sounds like a fantastic job for you. Plus, you and your brother would be working together."

My mother leaned forward and asked, "Are you sure that's something you want to do?"

"Maybe," I said as I circled the rim of my wine glass with my index finger. "It may not be exactly what I had in mind when I got my art degree, but it's still within the field."

"It's not a bad choice. And a job is a job, I guess," my mother muttered, leaning back in her chair.

"You don't seem too thrilled about it."

"I'm grateful that you have a job lined up. But being a sketch artist is a commitment, and a challenging one at that."

"Natalie said the same thing, but I can handle it. I may hear some disturbing details from people's violent encounters, and see some awful things, but I'll work through it."

"I agree," Bryan chimed in. "I'll probably see a lot more than she'll ever see during her time on the force. Plus, she has me, Natalie, and you guys to talk to whenever she needs to decompress."

"We don't even know if I'm going to get the job yet. It's just an interview."

My father gave me a grin that stretched from cheek to cheek. "Of course you're going to get it. The Danes can get anything they set their minds to."

"Thanks, Dad. I appreciate the encouragement."

My mother stood up, her plate in hand. "Why don't we have some dessert? I picked up a strawberry cheesecake from the local bakery."

We all agreed, and soon, we were cleaning off the dining room table to make room for the cheesecake.

The rest of the night went smoother than the last few meals we'd had together. There was still some tension between my mother and me, but we stayed civil, keeping our conversations brief. It was around ten when my brother and I exited our parents' home. Bryan walked alongside me to our respective vehicles, and he leaned against his car with both arms on the hood. "Your interview is on Monday at 8 a.m. by the way. I'll shoot you a text on Sunday for a reminder."

"Thank you for getting me this interview, Bry," I said.

"No worries. Just make sure you nail it, okay?"

"I'll do my best."

He gave me a bright smile. "I'll see you later. Have a safe ride home."

I gave him a short wave as I watched him climb into his car. As I mounted my scooter, I tucked my helmet over my head, adjusting it so it was tight. After my brother pulled out of the driveway, I followed suit and headed back to my apartment. The whole way back, I tried to brainstorm everything I had to do before my interview on Monday. One thing I was sure of— I was not prepared in the slightest.

Chapter 3

I spent the whole weekend writing up a new résumé since my old one was slightly outdated. I also put together a small portfolio of sketches I'd done over the last few years. Bryan wound up texting me like he said he would and told me who I was meeting with. The interview was with the police captain, Drew Baker, who'd been working at the precinct for quite some time. My brother mentioned a few interview techniques I should use during my time with the captain, like good eye contact, straightforward and concise answers, and non-verbal feedback. I figured those tips were universal interview techniques, but I thanked my brother for the help anyway.

I skimmed my closet, keeping a close watch on the time. It was still fairly dark out when I woke, but I was amped to get the day going. Rifling through the only three dress shirts in my closet, I decided on a jet-black blouse that fit snug against my body. I paired it with my charcoal-gray slacks and sleek black dress shoes. After getting dressed, I had a quick breakfast before making my way down to the precinct.

By the time I arrived, the sun was already out in full force, beating down on the streets of Miami. Clutching the strap of my messenger bag, I looked up at the cream-colored building that looked to be only a few stories tall. The butterflies were now fluttering wildly in the pit of my stomach as I made my way toward the entrance. I pushed the glass door open and walked into the spotless lobby of the police headquarters. There were only a few people meandering about the precinct. Most were uniformed officers, but there seemed to be a few civilians too, based on their casual clothing.

When I reached the front desk, a bald man in his tan police uniform and forest-green tie greeted me. "Good morning, ma'am. How may I help you today?"

"I'm here for a job interview with Captain Baker," I replied.

"Name?"

"Callie Dane."

The officer's fingers clacked against the keyboard as he searched on his computer. He hummed as his fingers crept to a halt. "I see that you're scheduled for 8 a.m. I'll print out a visitor badge, and you can head up to the third floor. I'll let the receptionist in homicide know you're coming up."

"Thank you," I said with a nervous smile.

He gave me a short nod as he handed me the visitor sticker that he'd printed. I peeled the back off and tossed it into a trash can near the elevators. As I waited for the elevator, I stuck the sticker onto my dress shirt, making sure it was secure. It didn't take long for the elevator doors to open, and I was on the third floor in no time. I barely approached the third-floor reception desk when the woman there said, "You must be the interviewee. Captain Baker is down the hall and to the right. You can't miss it."

I looked down the corridor she pointed to and gave her a quick thanks. As I made my way to the police captain's office, I checked the time on my phone. It was exactly eight o'clock. I breathed a sigh of relief, since I'd been known to run late. When I arrived at the office, two men were bickering about something that I probably didn't have a right to know. The husky man behind the desk, who I assumed was the captain, spotted me as I hung back at the door. It was suddenly silent as the two men turned their attention to me.

I cleared my throat, stepped further into the room, and said, "I'm Callie Dane. I'm here for an interview."

The man behind the desk looked up at the wall clock at the far end of the room. "Oh, right on time. Why don't you have a seat while I escort my detective out."

He stood from his desk, adjusting his thick-rimmed glasses before making his way to the door. The detective gave me a quick once-over, making me feel uneasy under his incredulous stare. But I'd be lying if I didn't say I checked him out too. He had coal-colored hair that was mid-length and tussled with style, a few strands hanging loosely around his face. He also had a trim-cut beard and piercing dark-brown eyes. Those eyes narrowed as the detective pushed past me to meet up with the captain by the door.

As they began chatting again, I tentatively sat in one of the leather-padded armchairs by Captain Baker's desk. I tried not to eavesdrop as the two men continued to murmur by the door. To distract myself, I glanced at a couple of trinkets on the captain's desk. One was a silver pendulum, and another was a bear dressed like a Miami-Dade officer. The conversation was cut short when Captain Baker grumbled, "We'll talk later."

I heard the office door slam shut before the captain shuffled back to his chair. He reached out a hand for me to shake and said, "Sorry about that. It's nice to meet you, Ms. Dane."

I shook his hand. "You as well."

"I hope you realize you won't be receiving any special treatment just because your brother works for us."

"No, I would never."

"I'm kidding," he said as he let out a hearty chuckle. "May I see your résumé and portfolio?"

I rummaged through my messenger bag and pulled out the folder I had put together for the interview. I handed it over to the captain, and he flipped through it quickly.

"Now, you know what the job is?" he asked as he placed the folder on his desk.

"It's for the forensic sketch artist position."

"Your brother didn't tell you that the position extends beyond that of a forensic artist?"

I furrowed my brow as I took in what he said. "Bryan failed to disclose that bit of information."

Captain Baker leaned back in his armchair, lacing his fingers together and resting them on the desk. "We'd love to have a full-time forensic artist on our team, but at this time, it's not plausible. We'd like members of the team, who are already established in law enforcement, to do forensic-art jobs on the side. It's easier on us, and with the lack of relevant cases, it'd be useless to hire someone whose sole duty is sketching criminals."

"So, I have no chance of getting this job?"

"I didn't say that. Your portfolio, résumé, and background

are exquisite, but you do lack basic police training and knowledge. If you'd be willing to take some law-enforcement courses along with your forty-hour training to become a forensic artist, we'd love to have you aboard in another area of the police force."

"What openings are there?"

"We're always looking for more officers, of course. But after looking over your résumé, I feel you'd fit better in the role of a dispatcher or police clerk. Ultimately, the choice is yours, but there's no chance of getting this job any other way."

Working with anything other than art was not what I'd had in mind. But at this point, I didn't have many choices. While mulling it over, I noticed Captain Baker's eyes soften as he looked at me.

"You are one of our top candidates right now. Though I can see your hesitancy in taking this position, we'd love to have you join our team. If you'd like, I can give you forty-eight hours to think about it before we move on."

"The training is free?" I asked.

"It is. It'll probably be two to three weeks of courses."

"You know what? I'll take it."

He looked taken aback, but a grin soon formed on his round face. "That's great to hear. But let me make this clear. Even though you'll be trained, that doesn't mean you'll automatically get the job. We still have a final evaluation of all our new trainees and applicants."

"That makes sense. But I'll do my best to come out on top."

"You sound like your brother."

I smirked. "I get that a lot."

He stood, extending his hand toward me once more. "I'll send you an email with information on your training. Good luck, Ms. Dane. I hope to see you back soon."

I sprang to my feet, shaking his hand firmly. "Me too."

Captain Baker handed back my folder before walking me to his office door. He opened it for me and waved me off, and I meandered back to the elevators. The meeting went surprisingly well, but the job position was unexpected. I just hope to nail the next portion of the interview and get a chance to show off my art skills in the future. Before I reached the elevators, a firm hand grasped my forearm, spinning me around to face a broad chest. I looked up to see Bryan giving me a questioning gaze.

"How'd it go?"

I glowered at him, shoving his shoulder. "It would have gone better if someone had told me that it wasn't just a forensic artist position."

"Ow," he grumbled with a mock frown. "To be fair, I knew you wouldn't consider the job otherwise. I had to tell you it was solely an art position— nothing more."

"It still would have been nice. At least I wouldn't have been staring at your captain like a deer in headlights."

"I'm sorry, Cal. Did you at least get the job?"

I breathed out a sigh. "Not yet. I still have to go through training, along with a final evaluation, to be considered."

He nudged my right shoulder with his fist. "You'll get it."

I glanced down the corridor beyond him, remembering something else. "Hey, do you know a detective with medium-length black hair, trimmed beard, and brown eyes?"

"That sounds like my partner, Marco Suárez. What about him?"

I cocked my head to the side. "That's your partner? He doesn't seem very friendly."

Bryan shrugged, crossing his arms. "He's not bad once you spend some time with him. He's just a workaholic who takes his job seriously. I doubt he even goes home most of the time."

"I saw him arguing with Captain Baker when I went in for my interview. He didn't seem too happy that I was there."

"I'm sure he was just feeling you out. He's a cool guy, I promise."

Those piercing brown eyes invaded my thoughts again, but I pushed them aside. "Well, I guess I'll let you get back to your duties."

Bryan pulled me into a quick hug. "See you later, little sis."

After we said our goodbyes, I left the precinct and headed back home to prepare for my next few weeks of coursework.

Chapter 4

My three weeks of grueling training were now officially over, and I could barely get out of bed. It wouldn't have been so bad if I was only learning how to construct faces and use digital tools outside of sketching, but they placed me in a couple of self-defense courses too. I felt tough and capable after learning how to defend myself, but it definitely wasn't what I thought I'd signed up for. I also had to learn about local laws, state laws, and federal laws, should I ever have to testify in a case. The laws themselves weren't too hard to follow, but I was bored out of my mind through the long classes. I just hoped I retained enough information to prove myself in this career.

I felt my bed shift underneath me. "Are you going to sleep this beautiful Saturday away?" It was Natalie's voice.

Without opening my eyes, I mumbled into my sheets, "Yep."

"Don't be that way. We finally have a day to hang out, and you're going to waste it by lying here like a fat house cat."

"I'm sorry, Nat. I just don't have the energy to go out today."

Natalie flopped down next to me, and I turned over to peek at her. Her hazel eyes were peering at me with a pointed expression. "I even set us up for something fun tonight."

"What might that be?" I asked, quirking an eyebrow at my unpredictable friend.

"A drawing class, but with a twist."

"What's the twist?"

"Wine. Two glasses per person."

"Of course you'd pick something that involves booze."

"But of course. You like drawing, and I like drinking. It's a win-win."

I lay back on my pillow. "I don't know."

Natalie turned on her side to face me better. Her slim index finger adorned with a bright-green acrylic nail reached out to bop me on the nose. A sly smile graced her lips as she murmured, "You have to go."

"Why?" I groaned.

"I already paid. Plus, it'll take your mind off of everything that's happened this past month."

"How much did you pay?"

"Thirty for each of us."

"We could have used that for groceries and had our own drink-and-sketch party."

"Where's the fun in that? Be adventurous every once in a while. With this, we get out of the house and meet new people."

"I already did, by trying to get this job."

"Wow, such a big change." Natalie tapped me on my side before rolling off my bed. "I'll give you an hour. Then, we'll get ready and hit up that sketch-and-wine workshop."

"I know you won't let this go, so fine. And, I'll take that whole hour," I grumbled as I sank back into my sheets.

"Great! You didn't have much of a choice anyway," Natalie said with a snicker as she exited my room, closing the door behind her.

I flipped over on my mattress, trying to get comfy so I could rest for the next sixty minutes. But I couldn't fully relax. All I could think about was my next meeting with Captain Baker. He said I was pretty much a shoo-in for the job opening, but I didn't want to get my hopes up. I was still disappointed that I wasn't even going to be a forensic artist, just an office worker until a case arose that may need my expertise. Who knew how long that would take? But maybe the extra income would help me build up enough savings to start up my own business for my art. It was worth a try. Besides, it's not like I had another choice at the moment.

Natalie and I sashayed down Ocean Drive, watching as the nightlife started to light up the dusk-cloaked avenue. We decided to dine out before going to our sketch-and-wine class, so we stopped at a local hotspot before heading to the gallery. The Art Deco architecture was always a joy to check out. The retro style pretty much dominated this area of Miami. Plus, the beach was right next door, giving the area a hip and lively atmosphere.

As we continued down the crowded sidewalks, I asked

Natalie, "Where is this thing being held?"

"The Creative Swatch Gallery," she answered.

"They have lovely art pieces there. I tried to get in once, but no dice. They weren't accepting new pieces at the time."

"You'll get in someday. Maybe they'll see your work tonight and personally invite you to display your art in their gallery."

I chuckled, rolling my eyes toward the sky. "That would be the dream."

We arrived a few minutes early, so we wandered around the gallery, admiring some of the paintings and photographs hanging on the walls of the first floor. Natalie cocked her head as we eyed a painting being showcased in the middle of the room. It comprised several different strokes of a brush with only a handful of colors. The red, blue, and green streaks didn't make a flattering picture, but it was "art" nonetheless.

"I still don't understand how they can this art. Your stuff would look way better here than this piece of junk," Natalie stated with a shake of her head.

I shrugged. "You know what they say, 'art is in the eye of the beholder.'"

"Whoever it is needs their eyes checked, because this is awful."

A man's voice came from behind us and said, "My optometrist said that my last prescription was fine."

We turned to face the man, who was wearing a bright-red dress shirt and dark pants. He had sandy-brown hair and thick-rimmed glasses that were a tad lighter than the shirt he wore. Natalie cleared her throat. "You're the artist, aren't you?"

"I am."

"I'm not one to apologize for stating the truth. So, I hope you can accept that I'm not a fan of your work."

"My work wasn't intended to be liked by everyone."

"I'm glad you realize that." Natalie grabbed my hand and said to the man, "If you'll excuse us, we have a class to get to."

We hustled toward the stairs, the artist following behind us. As we made our way to the second floor, stepping into the next section of the gallery, the man continued to pursue us. Natalie turned to face him when we reached the door to the workshop. "Why are you following us?"

He grabbed the handle, cracking the door open a smidge. "I'm the instructor."

Natalie plastered on a forced smile. "Of course you are."

"Grab a drink and take a seat. We'll be getting started soon."

Natalie sighed while I chuckled at her expense. We walked in, and I noticed that only a handful of spots were taken. Most attendees were women, but there were a few guys sprinkled into the mix. The two of us grabbed a glass of wine from the table set up in the back, a small cheese spread accompanying the bottles of red and white. We took the drinks to a table in the middle of the room and waited for the workshop to start. The layout was simple— an eleven-inch by fourteen-inch sheet of sketch paper with three drawing pencils for each participant. As the instructor wrote on the chalkboard in front of him, he said to the group, "My name is Dylan Hoyte. I've been a professional artist for over ten years and have been displayed in at least a dozen galleries all over the world. I don't expect you all to be on my level by the end of this, but I hope you take home some useful tips to improve your art a bit."

A woman raised her hand and asked, "Do you own this place?"

"I wish I did. I just help out when I'm in town. Three other Miami-based artists created this gallery fifteen years ago." He glanced around the room. "Any more questions before we get started?"

The room was silent. Dylan walked over to a table at the front of the room. On it stood a vase with a variety of flowers and some fruits in the foreground, all situated on top of a maroon cloth. He gestured to the objects and said, "As you can see here, I set up this little display so we can draw a still-life piece together. Now, you do not have to follow my techniques or draw this specific scene. You can choose anything in the room, or even a picture in your head. We're just here to have fun and drink some wine."

He settled at an easel propped in front of the table filled with colorful fruits and flowers. Dylan grabbed a pencil from the lip of the easel and said, "Let's get started, everyone."

After that, all that could be heard were the strokes of pencils gliding over the rough sketch paper. I fell into an artistic rhythm as I zoned out what was going on around me. Every time Dylan chimed in with his special techniques and tips, his voice sounded muffled in my ears. I was wholly focused on myself. It had been a while since I could relax and get into a good flow with my art style. Even though I'd been opposed to this impromptu girls' night, I was starting to think this was exactly what I needed after this crazy month. I felt like myself again. I connected with the passion for art that had been dwindling over the years, and it was great to get it back, even if only for today.

Halfway through drawing the vase and flowers, I got my other glass of wine that was included in the package. While I sipped at my glass, savoring the notes of oak and raspberry that coated my tongue, I looked over my half-complete work. My eyes wandered over to Natalie's artwork, and I sputtered on my wine. I nudged my friend in the arm. She peered over at me with a questioning gaze and asked, "What?"

"Are you kidding me? That's inappropriate," I whispered.

She rolled her eyes. "Don't be such a prude. It's not like we're in school and the teacher's going to send us to detention. Plus, it's art."

I shook my head, a smirk tugging at my lips. "If you say so."

"You'll like it once it's done. Maybe we can even hang it in our living room."

"You can hang it in *your* room."

"Fine."

I went back to my artwork, shading different sections and filling in more details on the fruit and flowers to add a textured look. While I was adding a few light touches to certain parts of the sketch, Dylan set his pencil down and said, "Our time is up, everyone. I hope you all enjoyed our little workshop today. I'll come around and check out each of your pieces before you get going."

As he went around the room, I looked over at Natalie's completed drawing. The male genitals were quite prominent on the page with details I didn't think she was capable of sketching. An embarrassed groan escaped me as I mumbled, "I can't believe you drew that."

"He said we could draw whatever we pictured in our heads. So I did." She tilted her head, eying her work with a suggestive smirk. "It's quite good, isn't it?"

"I'm actually surprised at the level of artistry you demonstrated here."

"I guess I've seen enough of them to draw one from memory."

Dylan finally made his way over to us. He viewed my

artwork first, not even noticing Natalie's lewd sketch. With a nod, he said, "Well done. You've got the focal point, clean lines, and fantastic use of shading. Are you an artist?"

"I went to college for it and got my degree. I'm still trying to get my foot in the door to create art on a professional level," I explained, fidgeting with my pencil.

"It took me five years to get to a level where I could sleep happily and not worry whether my bills would be paid. If there's one tip I can give you, it's don't give up on it. Take every job, no matter how small; it may lead to your big break."

"Thank you. I'll keep that in mind."

Dylan finally saw Natalie's drawing. A guttural chuckle rose from his throat as he looked it over. "I, too, am partial to that particular organ."

"Too bad. I was going to invite you back to my place and apologize for what I said about your work," she answered with a disheartened shrug.

"All is forgiven after seeing this. You two have a good night." He gave us a quick smirk before strolling over to the next two attendees.

We left the gallery with our sketches in hand. As we made our way to Natalie's clunker parked a few streets over, she lamented, "Man, I didn't think he was gay."

"Do you want to sleep with every man you meet?" I asked, suppressing a smile.

"Not everyone. But hey, I like to live life to the fullest and have new experiences."

"I don't know how you do it."

"Simple. I have no care in the world and look to have fun. In twenty years, I can reflect on the good times I've had. You should try it sometime."

I trained my eyes on the pavement. "I'll think about it."

"That's the problem. Don't think, just do. Like your art. I watched your process when we were sketching in there. You let it wash over you and take control. It's the same with life. Just let it happen and let your feelings flow."

I turned to her, raising an eyebrow. "I never thought you'd be the one giving out intellectual advice."

She giggled. "What can I say? I'm full of surprises. I also heard it on a TED Talk, or maybe a podcast. Either way, I can't take full credit for that wisdom."

"That makes more sense."

She wrapped her arm around me as we ambled to her car. "I think a few more glasses of wine are in order tonight."

"I don't know about that, Nat." When she gave me a narrowed look, I caved. "You know what, why not?"

She clapped with a squeal of victory. "That's the spirit."

The rest of the weekend flew by, and Monday now loomed over me. It was time to receive my final evaluation from Captain Baker. I was more nervous than I thought I'd be. I needed the money, and I'd already put tons of hours into having a shot at this job. While waiting for the captain, I sat in his office, second thoughts creeping into my mind. What if I wasn't good enough? I hadn't had much luck with my art so far. If I wound up landing a place on a case and botched a sketch of a suspect or victim, I'd be out of a job, again. Quite possibly not wanting to pick up a pencil or brush ever again. Maybe I was overreacting, but I knew my confidence was waning as my passion started to fail me. Before my mind could plague me with more disheartening thoughts, Captain Baker strolled into the room with a cheerful grin on.

"Sorry to keep you waiting, Ms. Dane. So, you still want the job?"

"Yes, I would like to take the police clerk position," I responded.

"I see you've taken all the necessary classes over the last couple of weeks. You seem to have done well enough in each one too," he said, studying his computer screen. "Okay, welcome aboard. I'll keep you in mind if we ever need a forensic artist, but be aware that those types of cases are few and far between."

"I appreciate it. I guess I just have to settle for where I am right now."

"Now, you won't be starting until tomorrow, but I thought you'd like to see your new work quarters. You'll also meet your new coworker, Mabel. She's a real gem. She's been working here almost as long as I have."

"I'd love to."

We took the elevator down to the first floor of the precinct. The captain showed me the small food court where I could get lunch or a snack, along with the nearest restrooms. After making our way down a few different halls, we stopped in front of a door with a black placard. It read, Room 105 – Records Room. Captain Baker opened the door for me, letting me step inside the cramped room first. There were two sections of a joint desk. Each one held a computer monitor, mouse, landline phone, and a few other office supplies.

A woman around my parents' age sat at the desk closest to the door. She raised a finger at us as she chatted on her phone. I took the chance to glance around the room. The anterior wall was lined with beige filing cabinets and a corkboard tacked with papers, its tray holding pens of multiple colors. Lastly, there were a couple of trash cans. It didn't seem like the coziest place to work, but it would have to do for now.

The woman, who I assumed was Mabel, hung up the phone and asked, "What can I do for you, Captain?"

"I want you to meet your newest recruit, Callie Dane. She'll be starting tomorrow. I thought you two should get acquainted. Maybe you can show her a few of the ropes before she gets started," he said.

The woman cast me a friendly glance, a sparkle in her eye. "Nice to meet you, sweet pea. I could use an extra pair of hands down here. I'm not getting any younger, that's for sure."

Captain Baker waved away her concern. "You're doing great, Mabel. You look younger than ever."

She shook her head with a chuckle. "Thanks, Captain."

"Well, I've got to get going. Good luck, Ms. Dane. I'm sure I'll be seeing you around." He waved goodbye to Mabel before exiting the room.

Mabel stood and shuffled up to me, reaching out a slender hand that was lacking the wrinkles I'd expected. I shook it, feeling the firm grip she had probably perfected over the years. She gave me a warm smile, revealing two middle teeth with a tiny gap between them. "Nice to meet you."

"You too," I said. "This is where I'll be working, huh?"

"Yep. You'll get used to it." She pointed to the rows of filing cabinets. "All of these are stuffed with case information and filed reports from over three and a half decades. Most of our newest stuff, spanning early 2006 to now, is on the computer. I'll show you how we import things and search information on our database tomorrow."

"Everything before 2005 is in these filing cabinets?"

"Oh, no. These go until the year 2000, if that. We have a whole other room that is packed to the brim with cabinets. We don't have to dig in there often, but occasionally, an old case pops up that needs to be pulled from the other room."

"Do you have a hard time finding things?"

"Not at all. Once I teach you the basics, you'll start going through the motions and figuring out how to do the work along the way."

I glanced down at a picture on Mabel's desk that was half-turned toward me. I pointed to the frame. "Is that your family?"

"It is. My two sons and their wives along with my five grandbabies, spread out between the two of them."

"They look lovely."

"They're the best. It was rough being a single parent when they were growing up, but they handled it like champs. I like to think I did too."

"I'm sure you were a great mom, and still are."

"Thank you. Do you have any family?"

I fidgeted with the hem of my shirt, clearing my throat. "My parents are still around. I also have a brother, who works here."

"I knew your last name sounded familiar. Is your brother Bryan?"

"It is. You know him?"

"I've met most people who work here. Your brother is quite a character. Real sweet too."

I smiled. "He's pretty cool when he wants to be. He helped me get this job, so I owe him, I guess."

She looked down at the thin silver watch on her wrist and said, "I hate to cut this short, but I have to get back to work.

I'll help set you up tomorrow and give you a better rundown on how we do things in here."

"Sounds good. It was nice meeting you, Mabel."

"You too, Callie. I'll see you tomorrow."

I gave her a curt nod before leaving the room. My new coworker seemed down to earth. She reminded me of some of my dads' relatives all mixed into one person. A dark, gloomy records room still isn't where I'd envisioned myself after college, but maybe this is a step in the right direction. I decided it wouldn't be so bad here after all, at least for a little while.

Chapter 5

The computer stalled as I tried to input the next report into the database. I groaned, throwing my head back until it hit the headrest of the dinky mesh chair. Mabel came over to our joint desk and dropped more files onto her already-large pile. She looked over at my computer and chuckled. "Wait until you experience the dreadful blue screen and have to redo everything from the beginning."

"Why don't we get new computers? These are, like, fifteen years old and they're barely functioning," I said as I slammed my finger on the spacebar.

"Believe me, I've been asking for years. Usually, I'm met with the age-old excuse of not having room in the budget. Other times, they tell me that once they fund another section of the headquarters, they'll look into updating our systems. Hasn't happened yet."

"That's not fair. You would think they'd make our office top priority since we manage the bulk of reports, claims, and information at the precinct."

Mabel shrugged, wandering over to her own computer. "You're right. It's not like we don't have the means to do it. I have a feeling they think we'll be out of commission longer than necessary with all the documents we'd have to transfer from the hard drives."

"Isn't most of it stored in the database?"

"Most of the new stuff is. But all the folders that are over ten years old are on the drives."

"Well, I hope they fix it soon, because it's taking me my whole shift to input two files."

"Tell me about it. I'm sure I'll be gone by the time they do finally update things."

I swung my chair to face her. "You're thinking about retiring?"

She shook her head with a small smile. "Not yet, but soon. I want to spend more time with my grandbabies and children before it's too late."

"I understand. I just hope I don't have to stay here long."

"I said the same thing many years ago, but here I am."

I slumped in my chair, feeling deflated. "Think I'll suffer the same fate?"

"No, I don't. You seem like someone who goes after what you want. Not that I didn't try, but nothing seemed to fall into place when I went to pursue another career." She leaned over and patted my arm reassuringly. "I'm rooting for you. Someone in this place needs to achieve their dreams, and it's not me. Not anymore."

"Thank you, Mabel."

Silence hung over our cluttered room as we got back to work. The only sound hitting my ears was the typing on our keyboards as we filled out our forms.

After five strenuous hours of work, it was finally lunch time. Once Mabel returned from her designated break, it was my turn to head out. I was halfway through the office door when my brother dashed over to me. He seemed out of breath as he fought out, "Cal. . . We need you."

"Need me? For what?" I watched as my brother gulped for air, resting his hands on his knees.

"We found a woman who was kidnapped a couple of weeks ago. She knows what her assailant looks like, and we need someone to sketch him out."

My heart skipped a beat as I processed his words. "Wait. . . You guys have a case for me?"

"Yeah, but we have to go now."

I glanced around, trying to get my bearings straight. "Let me tell Mabel so she doesn't worry."

I popped my head into the office and told my new coworker the good news. Mabel gave me two thumbs up and whispered, "Good luck."

Before I knew it, I was following my brother to the elevators. As we waited, I turned to Bryan. "Why were you so out of breath?"

He pressed the elevator button and said, "The elevator was taking too long, and I didn't want you to miss out on this opportunity. So I ran down three flights of steps to get to you."

A smile tugged at my lips. "Thank you for thinking of me,

Bry."

"I know how much you'd rather be doing art than filing reports. When I heard this opportunity arise, I knew you had to take it."

"I just hope my work will be good enough."

"Don't worry about that. Just do the best you can."

I nodded, feeling determined. "I'll try."

The elevator finally arrived, taking us to our destination within seconds. Bryan led me to a room where his partner and Captain Baker were standing outside the door. Captain Baker dipped his head to me and asked, "Do you think you'll be able to do this?"

"It was the main reason I wanted to work here. I'm up for the challenge," I replied, holding my chin high.

"That's what I like to hear." He turned to my brother and his partner and added, "You two give her a brief rundown before sending her in. Got it?"

"Yes, sir," the two mumbled before the captain stalked away to his office.

I looked up at the two men and asked, "Besides being a kidnapping victim, what else do I need to know?"

Marco glanced through the glass window to the interview room, surveying the victim. "Her name is Wendy McCann. Her sister filed a missing-person report two weeks ago when she didn't return to their shared apartment after her shift at work. This morning, Wendy was found at a gas station forty miles from where she was last seen, and now she's here."

Bryan chimed in, "She's still pretty shaken up. Be cautious with her, and make her feel as comfortable as you can. We need every piece of information we can get if we want to nab her abductor."

I studied the young woman whose head was hung low as she continued to wait. "I took some courses on cognitive interviewing, and I'd like to think I'm pretty empathetic. I should be able to pull this off."

Marco huffed, his eyes boring into mine. "I hope so. We can't afford a dead end in this. A detailed sketch of the assailant will be the icing on the cake to catch this son of a bitch. That is, if your art skills are as good as they say."

"Lay off her, Marco," Bryan grumbled as he side-eyed his partner. "She can do this. It's not like we have many other choices right now anyway. Besides, it wouldn't be the first time we had to solve a case without a sketch."

Marco didn't say another word as he marched away from us, shaking his head. I turned to my brother. "Nice guy, huh?"

"These types of cases aren't his favorite, for personal reasons. That makes him a little more aggressive. But it's not my story to tell," Bryan said.

I stole another glance through the window. "I guess I should get started with my interview."

"Yes. I'll bring the tools you need. While you wait, chat with Wendy and build a rapport with her so she warms up to you."

I nodded and then slipped into the interview room. My stomach twisted into knots. Was I in over my head by taking this job? It was starting to feel like it. The girl looked up at me as she sniffled quietly. Her chestnut hair was draped over her face, obscuring her eyes. I sat across from her in one of the metal chairs, far enough to give her some space but close enough so we could hear each other.

"Hi, Wendy. I'm Callie. It's nice to meet you," I said while trying to keep my nerves at bay.

"Are you another detective?" she asked as she pushed her

hair back.

Her hazel eyes were puffy and red, probably from crying. Her swollen left eye was a nasty mix of purple and black. She also had a cut on her lip that seemed to be healing.

"I'm not a detective. I'm a police clerk who's trying to become a forensic artist," I said.

"Is that like a sketch artist? The ones who do those rough drawings of suspects and missing people?" she asked.

"It is."

"That's pretty cool. I always wanted to draw, but the best I can do is little flowers." She glanced away shyly.

"Everyone starts somewhere. I've been drawing since I was a kid, but this is definitely not where I thought I'd bring my talents."

"Where did you hope to be?"

I hummed as I sat back in my chair, pondering her question. "I wanted to have my own gallery or at least have a few pieces in someone else's gallery. How about you?"

A smile crept onto her face as her eyes shifted down to her hands in her lap. "It's probably a bit childish, but I wanted to be a ballerina. I spent years training. Then, I blew out my knee during my senior year after landing wrong on a jeté."

"That's not childish at all. I'm sure some people think my dream is childish as well. But the truth is, they're both valid careers, just as much as being an accountant or a police officer."

The door opened, and the shades on it clinked against the glass as it came to an abrupt halt. Bryan shot us a sympathetic smile as he brought over a sketchpad and a facial identification catalog. "I'm sorry to interrupt. I just wanted to drop this off for you, Callie."

Wendy glanced between us and asked, "Are you two related?"

"I'm her older brother," Bryan replied.

"By four years. But at least I got the good looks," I said, hoping to ease the girl's nerves a bit. Maybe my own as well.

"Your relationship reminds me of my sister and me." She chuckled, but it soon trailed off, a deep frown replacing her smile. "I miss her."

Bryan plastered on a cheery smile. "I got a hold of her. She said she'll be here soon."

"Really?" Her eyes widened.

"Yes." He started for the door. "I'll let the two of you continue. The faster you get the sketch done, the faster you can go home."

"Thank you, Detective."

Once Bryan left the room, Wendy and I were alone once again. I flipped open the empty sketchbook he'd dropped off and picked up a pencil. "Are you ready to describe everything that happened?"

"I guess so. I just want to get this over with so I can forget about this ordeal altogether."

"Then let's start from the beginning."

Three hours later, and I was barely halfway done drawing our perpetrator. It was coming along nicely, but we still had a lot of ground to cover. "Do you think you can go backward with what happened to you?"

"Backward? I can try," Wendy said, her left leg bouncing up and down.

"Take your time. We're in no rush."

She closed her eyes and lifted her head slightly. "I was at the gas station, trying to get help from the worker behind the counter. Before that, I was in a warehouse by the docks. I could smell the salty ocean water in the air and hear the seagulls' calls echoing around the buildings. I was tied up in an unmarked building. It was rundown and smelled like mildew."

"Before that?"

"The man came in to feed me a few times. Nothing fancy. Usually soggy sandwiches, like ham and cheese, or turkey." Her eyes shot open, and she said, "He had a tattoo on his wrist!"

"A tattoo?" I leaned forward, my nerves prickling.

"Yeah. I remember peeking at his arm when he handed me the sandwiches. His long-sleeved shirt rode up, showing a tattoo on his wrist."

I turned to another page on the sketchpad and asked, "Can you describe it to me?"

"It was simple. It looked like two Ls, but one was upright, while the other was flipped down. Both attached at the bottom ends."

She held up her hands in a U and twisted her right hand down to mirror the double L shape. I started to sketch out what she was trying to show me. "Were they thin lines, or an outline?"

"They were bold, spanning most of his wrist and lower arm."

I nodded as I continued to color in the L's that I had drawn. Once I was done, I turned the sketchbook towards Wendy and asked, "Is this it?"

"That's perfect," she said, looking it over.

"Great." I flipped the page back to the man we were

creating. "Want to get back to him?"

"Yes, let's finish him up." She drew a deep breath. "He smiled a couple of times as he tried to talk to me. I remember he had a small chip on his front left tooth. A hint of a beard on his face. . . It could have been a five o'clock shadow for all I know. He also had a couple of beauty marks, one on his cheek on the top left, by his eye. He had another on the right of his chin."

I scribbled in those details as I worked the pencil over the textured paper. Wendy was silent as I continued drawing, fleshing out what she had described over the last few hours.

"Stop," she said, placing a hand on top of mine to still my movements. "That's him."

I stared down at the balding man I'd created. His eyes were squinted in a menacing glare, his lips parted and the chip on his tooth prominent. "Are you sure this is him?"

"I've never been more positive in my life."

"I'll hand these sketches over to the detectives so they can look over them. And I'm sure they'll review the tapes to hear the full interview."

I started to get up, but Wendy grabbed my hand to stop me. "Do you think they'll catch him?"

The hope in her eyes had my heart aching for the poor girl. I didn't know the answer, but I wanted to reassure her as best I could. "I don't want to give you false hope. But knowing my brother, he'll do his best to bring you justice. His partner seems to be that way too."

When I exited the interview room, I drew a shaky breath, the horrors of the girl's story playing through my mind. As I rounded a corner, I spotted my brother at one of the desks in the bullpen. Wandering over to him, I placed my sketchpad on his desk. He looked up at me and asked, "How'd it go?"

"Not bad." I took a seat in the chair next to his desk. "I think I bit off more than I could chew. Maybe Natalie and Mom were right. I don't know if I can handle this."

"Come on, Cal. Don't do this to yourself."

"I can't help it. I spent four hours with a woman who was kidnapped, beaten, and left to die in an abandoned warehouse. The details. . . The details were awful, and all I wanted to do was cry for her."

He placed a comforting hand on my knee, his eyes locking on mine. His brown eyes shone with empathy as he said, "But you didn't do that. You kept it together. You have no idea how many times I wanted to break down during a case. There were even a few times I had to leave a room because I needed to catch my breath and recuperate."

"Will it ever get easier?" I asked, my eyes welling up.

"I'd love to say it does, but there are still cases that'll shock me. It may get a tad better, but there are still some days I want to curl up in bed with a bottle of whisky and weep for the victims."

I brushed away the few tears that escaped. "Why didn't you tell me?"

"It's something I wanted to deal with myself. I didn't want to drag you into it."

"If you ever need to get something off your chest, you know I'm here for you."

"I know, as am I. We'll always have each other, no matter what." Bryan picked up the sketchbook and flipped between the two sketches. "These are great, Cal. I'm sure these will help us get to the bottom of this case."

"I'm glad. I want Wendy to get her happy ending."

"Me too." He stopped on the tattoo again, tapping it with his index finger. "This looks familiar. I'm going to have to ask Marco if he recognizes it."

"Recognizes what?" Marco sauntered into the room, fixing the button on his charcoal-gray suit jacket.

Bryan handed my drawing over to Marco, who snatched it quickly. "Where did she see this?"

"On the man's wrist," I fumbled out.

"If this is what I'm thinking it is, we have to do some more digging."

Bryan scrunched his eyebrows, eyeing his partner. "Why?"

Marco glanced at me and said, "I'd rather not talk in mixed company."

I stood from my chair and mumbled, "I'll head out. My shift is technically over anyway."

As I started walking away, Bryan called out, "I'll call you later."

I gave him a short nod before heading to the elevators. As I waited, I figured out the first thing I was going to do when I got home— pop open a fresh bottle of wine and soak in a hot bath.

Chapter 6

While I was inputting information of a civilian who'd recently paid some fees that he owed the department, the office phone rang. Mabel picked up the line and spoke intermittently to the person on the other end. Finally, she said, "Hold on a moment. I'll let her know."

She put the phone on hold and swiveled her chair toward me. "It's the captain. He wants to talk to you."

I stared at the phone on my desk, wondering what he'd be contacting me about. Was this about my first sketch? Was there a new case? Was I going to be fired? I hesitantly picked up the phone, my mind still racing with questions. I clicked it off of hold and said, "Yes, Captain Baker?"

"I need you to come up to the third floor, Ms. Dane. We'll be in the briefing room," he rumbled.

I didn't even have time to respond before the line went

dead. When I hung up, Mabel asked, "What was that about?"

"Beats me. All he said was to come up to the third floor and meet them in the briefing room," I explained as I got up from my chair.

"Do you think it's another forensic art job?"

"I wouldn't think so. I only had my first case two days ago," I said, my throat dry and nerves skittering.

"Well, I'm sure it's nothing. I'll see you in a bit."

I hurried to the third floor, asking the receptionist where the briefing room was located. It wasn't hard to find once she directed me to the room. When I made my way inside, I was shocked to see almost every seat was taken except for one empty chair next to my brother. Captain Baker noticed me and gestured to the empty chair. "Have a seat, Ms. Dane."

I did as he said, and Bryan whispered, "What are you doing here?"

I shrugged. "No clue."

Captain Baker brought up a slide on the screen that hung in front of the room. There was a picture of Wendy and another one of her sister. The captain planted both of his hands on the long meeting table we were all occupying. As he braced himself on the hardwood tabletop, he said in an informative tone, "As you all may know, Wendy and her sister, Josephine, were murdered this afternoon."

An audible gasp left my lips. Everyone looked at me, making me slink down in my chair. The captain cleared his throat, pulling all eyes back to him at the front of the room. "We have reasons to believe that Wendy's kidnapping and the recent murder of her and her sister were gang-related. Here's the weird part. Our suspected criminal, Esteban Rojas, featured in this sketch by our forensic artist, Callie Dane, is also dead."

The slide switched to the two sketches I'd done. One showcased the suspect and the other, his tattoo. The captain crossed his arms. "Now, we'd love to close the case once all pertinent information has been gathered, but we have one more situation. The gang tied to this, Lucifer's Losers, has been growing in number and wreaking more havoc in our community."

"What's this have to do with anything? We've never gone after a whole gang before," Marco grumbled, leaning his elbows on the table.

"My niece, Amber Oliva, has been linked to this gang multiple times. Last week, her parents got a cryptic text from her that made it sound like she was in trouble. It's not unusual for her not to show up at home or school for a couple of days here or there. But no one has heard from her or seen her since that text."

A man with short red hair who sat across from me raised his hand. Once called on, he asked the captain, "Does that mean we're doing this for personal reasons?"

Captain Baker shook his head. "No. We're doing this to protect the other fifteen to seventeen-year-olds who are getting recruited into this gang. If we can chip away at this group from the inside, we might be able to put a stop to them, at least for a while."

Marco spoke again. "Who are we sending in?"

"This is the challenging part. Our team has been breached, and no one knows how far it goes. If the gang catches wind of our plans or recognizes one of our people, that's game over. It could even mean the death of a team member."

"Then what are we going to do?"

"We're going to get someone outside of the field to go undercover to be our informant." The captain looked dead at me. "Callie Dane, our police records clerk and occasional sketch artist."

Before I could say anything, Bryan jumped to my defense. "You want my sister to join a gang?"

"She won't be joining it, Detective Dane. Not directly." Captain Baker put up another picture with some lines of information on the screen. "After all the digging you and Detective Suárez did, we found that the warehouse where Wendy was kept is a front for the gang. They own a loading dock and part of a cargo port near South Beach."

Bryan leaned back, his mouth agape. "Are you thinking they're shipping out more than just products?"

"Yes, I do. I also think they're bringing things in. If we get to the bottom of their operations, we can report to the FBI and DEA with our findings."

"I don't know about this, Captain. This seems like a longshot, not to mention potentially dangerous."

Marco nodded approvingly. "I think it's a great idea. With her art background, I'm sure she can draw us up some detailed sketches of key players and gather valuable information. We can also monitor her during her time there."

The captain dipped his head in agreement. "Exactly. But the choice is up to Callie."

Eyes were back on me as I tried to contemplate this new ordeal. Bryan was right—this was dangerous. I barely had the training to file closed cases. How was I going to infiltrate a gang? With a sigh, I looked up at the captain and said, "I signed up to sketch criminals, not catch them."

"Well, you won't necessarily be doing the apprehending.

You'll be gathering intel for us to catch these guys."

I chewed at my plump bottom lip in contemplation. The captain certainly seemed to have faith in me. "Do I have time to think about it?"

Captain Baker glanced at the watch on his wrist and said, "I'll give you twenty-four hours to mull it over. Detective Suárez, Detective Dane, meet me in my office with Callie tomorrow at noon. Everyone is dismissed."

As the officers and detectives dispersed, leaving the briefing room one by one, Bryan stayed behind with me. "Cal, you're not actually considering this, are you?"

"I'm divided. It could be an interesting way to break into the business, and maybe they could open a permanent sketch artist job for me. On the other hand, I could be targeted by an aggressive gang, and get myself killed," I said as I weighed my options.

"Look, you're an adult. I can't tell you what to do, but whatever you choose, I'll support you. If you decide to go out there, I'll do everything in my power to keep you safe."

I pulled my brother into a quick hug. "I know you would. I just need time to think this through."

"Take your time on this one. This is a serious decision. Once you're in, you can't pull out."

"I'm aware, Bry. Believe me, I'm going to spend the next day thinking about this from every angle."

"That's good to hear," he said. He started heading for the door before turning back to me. "If you want to run anything by me, don't hesitate to call."

"I'll keep that in mind."

He gave me a forced smile, the uneasiness of the situation shining in his eyes. I knew he didn't want me to do this, but something about the case intrigued me. What if I could help take down an organization that killed two innocent women? Wendy and her sister deserved justice, and if I was one of the only people who could get it for them, then maybe I would.

I took the rest of the day off from work to ponder the task I was given by Captain Baker. There were so many reasons not to do this undercover sting, but only one reason in favor of it— justice for those women and any other victims the gang may have targeted. I could also benefit from the experience, but there was no guarantee that the department would offer me a full-time position as a forensic artist to reward my work.

As I lounged on the couch, picking at the small tear that had formed on the headrest, Natalie strolled through the door. She examined me as she crept toward the couch and perched on our crowded coffee table. "Sweatpants, disheveled hair, and a look of despair. Something's wrong."

I explained the whole situation to Natalie, from the beginning to the present moment. She nodded along to the whole story until I finally asked, "What do you think I should do, Nat?"

"That sure is a predicament you got yourself into." She lifted my legs and plopped down next to me before laying them across her lap. "Honestly, I think you should do it."

"Because you would do it?"

"Well, duh. Do you know how many crime shows and true-crime documentaries I've seen with those types of high-stakes scenarios? If you do it, I get to live vicariously through you."

"Does it usually work out in those shows?"

"For the most part. There was this one time when this undercover cop was found smooth. . . You know what, never mind."

I suppressed a shudder. "Maybe I should reconsider."

"I'm sure nothing bad will happen to you. Your brother is on the force, and they seem competent enough. Remember that time I was arrested for drunk and disorderly? The officers were on top of everything."

I sat up and said, "How can I forget? I was the one who bailed you out, and it wasn't even with my own money. I still owe Bry two thousand bucks, which you owe me."

Natalie's eyes widened. "Oh, right. You know, about that. I'll get it to you eventually."

I rolled my eyes and waved it off. "Don't worry about it."

After a short silence, Natalie murmured, "So, what are you going to do?"

"Not a clue." I stumbled off the couch and stretched my stiff limbs. "I'm going to sleep on it. Hopefully by tomorrow afternoon I'll have an answer."

Chapter 7

Still contemplating my decision with only minutes to spare, I was ninety-five percent sure I would take the undercover job. Even though this was pretty far outside of my domain, it beat sitting around in a clustered office space all day, filling out paperwork and taking payments from civilians. When I reached Captain Baker's office, he was already sitting at his desk, probably awaiting my arrival. Bryan and Marco were there too. Bryan was sitting in front of the captain's desk while Marco leaned against the back wall with his arms folded.

"Come in, Ms. Dane," Captain Baker as he gestured me inside. "Close the door so the four of us can chat in private."

I latched the door closed behind me before taking the seat next to Bryan. He looked at me expectantly as I announced, "I decided to take the job. I'll go undercover and be an informant for the MDPD."

Captain Baker's eyebrows came together in a serious expression. "Are you certain? Once this case starts, there is no turning back. We have to see this through whether we collect enough evidence for prosecution or not. And this can be highly dangerous for you too."

"I understand that, Captain. I will take this job seriously and won't back out."

Bryan looked over at me, and I could see a hint of fear in his eyes. "Callie. I'm not so sure about this."

"Trust me, Bry. I can do this. And I know you'll have my back."

He clenched his jaw, his eyes sparking with determination. "I will. I won't let anything happen to you."

"You Danes have guts, I'll tell you that," Captain Baker said as he glanced between us. He took out a manila folder, opening it up on his desk. It was stuffed with papers and photographs that I figured were pertinent to the case at hand. "You'll be going undercover as a warehouse worker at Conwell's Oceanic Shipping Company. You'll be sent in for an interview on Friday with a man named Jay Housten. He's a low-level thug who screens new employees."

"I have to do a job interview?" I asked, my voice rising.

"We want you to be the most authentic new employee they get, so yes. I could pull some strings to get you in, but that'd ring up red flags. They're already suspicious of us. We don't need to give them any more reason to be."

"I guess we don't want my cover blown before we even start."

"Exactly. Okay, moving on. You'll be going undercover as Callie Duncan. We kept most of your information the same, except for any details that could be traced back to your real identity. Spruced up your résumé a bit too. Wanted you to have a little experience with warehouse work."

"What will I be doing while I'm there?"

"Collecting intel, for starters. Anything you see or hear, jot it down, even if it doesn't seem important. Also, with your expertise in art, I'd like you to sketch out some people you may find suspicious or who need looking into. It could be useful."

"Who runs this company?"

"It used to be Vince Conwell. He built this company from the ground up thirty-seven years ago. Ten years ago, he died in a mysterious plane crash over the Pacific Ocean. Everyone on board perished."

"Who runs it now?"

"His daughter, Kris Conwell. Not much is known about her. She keeps her head down and doesn't seem to be one for the spotlight. I'm sure she pushes most of her dirty deeds onto her lackeys, much like her father did when he was alive."

"Are we sure he isn't still alive?"

Marco snorted in the back of the room, making me crane my head toward him. "You've seen one too many movies. Even though fake deaths do happen, it's very rare. As far as we know, Vince is dead, and Kris is pulling the strings he left her."

"That's right," Captain Baker said. "We have no reason to believe that Mr. Conwell could be alive."

I turned back to the captain and asked, "Do I have to meet this Kris lady?"

"Well, if you can get to her, it'll make our jobs easier. You're going to be dealing with low-level criminals, maybe a few high-level ones, but the top is going to be hard to touch. If we start taking them out from the bottom, we could make our way up the ladder and pin this whole operation on the Conwell family, destroy their dirty business."

"This seems like a long-term operation," I said, my throat suddenly dry.

"If things are done right, it shouldn't take more than a month, but I have seen undercover jobs take years. Some don't have a desirable outcome, even after all the time and effort put into them."

"Oh. . ."

"There's still time. Want to back out?"

I shook my head. "No. I want to do this for Wendy, her sister, and your niece. The gang needs to be stopped."

"It's always good to know who you're doing this for and why you're doing it. I always felt that it gave me more strength to stick with this job, no matter how painful it gets."

"Anything else before I go?"

"Your interview is on Friday at 10 a.m. You'll be meeting at the local office by the docks near South Beach. Don't be late."

"I won't, sir."

"I want you checking in with me, Marco, and Bryan once you start at the job site. Emails and impromptu meetings here at the precinct will be essential. While you're collecting intel, we'll get working on any new information you find so we can continue our investigation. It'll be a never-ending cycle until this case is done." Captain Baker grabbed a yellow envelope and handed it to me. "I almost forgot. This has all the details regarding your new identity and some basic info that we went over today. Study it before your interview so you're familiar with your new self and place of employment."

I peeked inside, noticing a thick packet along with some other papers and materials. "I'll try to get through it."

"It's not as long as it looks, I promise. I'll see you on

Saturday for a briefing."

"See you then," I said, trying to sound confident. When Bryan stood with me to leave, Captain Baker eyed him. "I need you and Marco to stay here for a moment. I have some things I want to discuss with you two."

"Can I have a quick minute with my sister?" he asked.

"Sure. You have one minute."

Bryan led me out of the room, closing the door behind him. "Please be careful, Cal. This is nasty stuff you're getting into."

"I know that, Bryan. I'll do my best."

"I'm sure you will. You're a Dane, after all." He gave me a weak smile as he embraced me, squeezing me tight. "I'll see you later. If you need anything, and I mean anything, reach out to me. Okay?"

"You'll always be the first person on my list."

"I better be." He gave me a cheesy wink before heading back into the office.

As I wandered out of the station, I continued to dig through the envelope I was given. I wasn't keen on homework, but if I didn't brush up on the information I received, it could bring the investigation to its knees before it even started. It looked like my week would be spent learning some new stuff.

On the day of my interview, my mind kept running back to the information I received about Conwell's company. There wasn't much to go on besides who owned it, potential suspects, and the products they imported, both illegal and legal. The only thing I had to memorize was my new identity and what she has been doing for the last couple of years. Apparently, I'd been jumping from job to job as a maid, janitor, and even a grocery stocker. It wasn't as difficult as I thought it'd be, and I'd had time to read through everything twice before my interview today. I had no idea what to wear. Since this wasn't a corporate job, I didn't want to look overly put together. But I didn't want to look like a slob either. With help from Natalie, we decided on a simple black dress shirt and dark jeans. Casual, yet professional. Once I was ready, I headed down to the docks for my interview, arriving five minutes early.

As I strolled up to the office building, which stood a few streets away from the loading docks, I tried to survey the area. It looked like normal Miami. Traffic, shirtless men, and palm trees. I could even hear the seagulls squawking as they flew around the coastal port. I caught a glimpse of the warehouse I'd be working at, but the angle of the street made it difficult to get a clear view. From afar, it seemed like a normal business with cargo and pallets being hauled from place to place. Some workers were in safety gear while others wore bright-orange shirts and caps. The workplace didn't raise any red flags, but I was sure that's how they'd been getting away with their shady deeds for so long.

Upon entering the office, it was apparent that they didn't utilize the building for much. There were a few windows, about five chairs, a couple of tables with magazines, and a reception desk at the front. They probably only used this space for interviews, and maybe a few other company affairs. I spotted one other person in the small waiting room, reading a magazine from the table. I made my way up to the reception desk where a younger man with a buzzcut greeted me with a half-smile. "Name's Rodger. Are you here for the job interview, ma'am?"

"Yes. My name is Callie Da—Duncan," I said, catching

myself from giving my real name.

Rodger typed something into the computer, and I noticed the tattoo on his left hand. It was the same design Wendy described, what the MDPD identified as the Lucifer's Losers gang symbol. I tried to make a detailed mental note of the young man so I could relay the information to the captain and sketch him out later.

"You're right on time, but Mr. Housten is running a bit late today. You'll go after the gentleman over there," he said, motioning to the other interviewee in the room. "It shouldn't be long, though. You can have a seat and read some magazines if you want."

"Thank you," I said before sitting in a chair across the room from the other man.

Rummaging through the magazines, I noticed that most of them were from ten years ago. I guessed the place didn't care about keeping up to date, which made sense. There weren't any major events going on here in the first place, so why pay for a useless subscription most people probably wouldn't read? I picked out an old *National Geographic* magazine and idly flipped through it. As I continued to wait, I pulled out my phone to jot down some of my thoughts about the place. I also wrote down Rodger's facial features so I could sketch him out later.

After twenty minutes, it was finally my turn to see Mr. Housten. Rodger led me to the backroom and gestured for me to sit in the ripped chair across Mr. Housten's desk. The dank room could have used a ton of TLC, but they obviously didn't have a reputation they wanted to uphold. Jay Housten wasn't at all how I'd pictured him. The gangly man had sunken eyes with heavy bags drooping beneath them. His hair was slicked back, making him appear older than he probably was. He looked like he'd had a rough life. His clean suit and perfectly straightened tie seemed to counteract the rest of his ragged appearance.

"Ms. Duncan, it's nice to meet you," he said.

"You too, Mr. Housten," I replied.

"Why are you here today?"

"I'm here for a job."

"Yes, but why this job? This doesn't seem like something you'd want to do. Your résumé indicates to me that you'd be better off somewhere else."

"I was let go from my last job and needed something quick to tide me over. The bills won't pay themselves," I tried to joke.

Mr. Housten didn't even crack a smile as he maneuvered papers around his desk. "It is rough, trying to find more qualified jobs down here in Miami. If money's tight, it makes sense to jump at the first opportunity you see."

"Yep. Those were my thoughts."

"Do you think you can do this? You'll be moving fifteen- to twenty-five-pound boxes for about nine hours every day. The warehouse can get quite demanding."

"I'm willing to put in the work. I can handle heavy boxes and whatever else may be thrown my way. I'm sure I could also ask for help as well."

"Hmm. . . A person who can ask for help. That's very rare here, but that's because most of our employees are men who think they're a bunch of tough guys. Lost a large pallet once because some young guy thought he could handle the lift without help, a friggin' disaster that was."

"Sounds bad."

"It was. Spent a whole day cleaning the mess, having shipments backed up, running behind." The man shrugged and added, "Don't matter, though. It was all dealt with. Back to you. We are trying to bring in more diversity here at the shipping company. Of course, we don't get many women signing up here, especially in this sector."

"That's not too shocking. This wouldn't necessarily be my first choice either, but a job is a job right now."

"Well said. So, if you want this position, it's yours."

I raised my eyebrows, a little taken aback. "That's it?"

"Yes indeed. What do you say, Ms. Duncan?"

"I'll take it."

He gave me an emotionless grin before getting up from his seat. Jay walked over to a file cabinet in the back corner of the room, opening up a couple of the top drawers. He rifled through each one as if searching for something. He pulled out one of those bright-orange outfits that I saw earlier and handed it to me. "Small is the best we got. It should fit you, but it might be a little big. There's a hat in there too."

I scrutinized the hideously colored uniform and said, "I'm sure that'll be fine."

"Get some tan cargo pants and a pair of sneakers to round the outfit out. Don't matter the color of the sneakers, but white is preferred."

"I'll make sure to get those."

"Great. You start Monday at 8 a.m. Don't be late. I'll let your manager know you're coming. He'll fill you in on the rest when you get there."

"Thank you, Mr. Housten."

"No problem. Welcome to the team, Ms. Duncan."

I shook the man's hand before leaving his office. My undercover job was officially underway. Luckily, I had a whole weekend to prep for this big experience. Despite my excitement, I was starting to feel a tinge of regret for taking on this project. At least I had another meeting with the captain, Marco, and Bryan tomorrow. I was sure they'd help ease my nerves. But would that be enough to keep me on track when the logical part of my brain was telling me to wuss out?

Chapter 8

I adjusted the cheap orange cap on my head as I gazed at my new uniform in the mirror. The matching polo shirt was baggy on my small frame while my tan cargo shorts fit snug on my wide hips. I paired the uniform with basic white sneakers that I'd found buried under a pile of clothing in my train wreck of a closet. The thought of going undercover made my palms sweat, but I was also worried about this fake job. No one else at the loading dock knew that I was working for the MDPD. I had to prove myself to two parties so I wouldn't get fired from either.

As I walked into the kitchen, Natalie was rinsing a bowl in the sink. The moment she saw me, she let out a howl of laughter. "Oh my gosh, you look ridiculous."

I tugged at the oversized shirt, and asked, "Is it that bad?"

"You look like a teenage boy who's going to skip school to

go spray graffiti under an overpass."

"This was a bad idea."

"At least it's temporary. I'm sure you won't be undercover for too long."

"I hope so." I grabbed a blueberry muffin from its plastic container and bit into it. "I just feel like I made the wrong decision. What if I blow my cover? What if I can't gather any evidence?" I said through a mouthful of tangy pastry.

Natalie placed a reassuring hand on my shoulder. "You'll do fine. You're the most observant and smartest person I know. You're going to make the police department wish they'd put you on their team sooner."

"Thanks for the encouragement."

"Any time, girl." She sauntered toward the door and said, "I'll see you tonight. I'll want to hear all about your first day."

"I'll give you the scoop when I get back."

A wide grin spread across her face before she headed out the door. With a glance at the hour on my phone, I scarfed down the rest of my muffin before heading off to my "new job."

I had to park my scooter in the garage one street over from the warehouse loading docks. Crossing the early-morning traffic and dodging the cyclists who were out for a scenic ride already had me groaning. I passed a few food trucks that were parked near our facilities as I made my way there. That's probably what most of the employees did for lunch, so I guess that's where I'd be heading this afternoon. They weren't my typical lunch choices, but they'd do. The three food trucks served up BBQ, fish, and a combination of burgers and pizza.

When I finally found my way inside the loading dock, a bald, stocky man waddled up to greet me. He was puffing on a cigarette, his arms folded across his chest. "You the new chick?"

"Yes, I'm Ca—"

"Don't care about your name. I'm Ted, your manager. The less we interact with each other, the better. So quick rundown, you get two ten-minute breaks, one at ten and one at five. You have lunch from one to one-thirty. Your shift ends at seven. Got that?"

"Yes. . ."

"Good. You'll be unloading and loading boxes over at station B. If you need any help, ask JC, the supervisor of your station. Any questions?"

"Well, I—"

"Ask JC."

He threw his cigarette on the ground, stomping it out with his wheat-colored work boot. As he walked away, I was left trying to find station B by myself. A faded letter on the upper corner of each loading dock helped lead me to my assigned station. Glancing around, I spotted a thin white man with short brown hair rummaging through a box on a metal table. I shuffled over to him and asked, "Are you JC?"

He chuckled as his hazel eyes peered down at me and shook his head. "No, I'm Ivan. You must be new."

"Is it obvious?"

"Oh yeah."

"Where can I find JC?"

He turned to a truck that was pulled up to the loading bay and pointed a calloused finger to an African-American man with a short afro. I gave my thanks to Ivan before making my way over to JC. He stopped moving boxes to look me over. "You Callie?"

"That's me," I answered.

"You don't seem like you can lift much."

I forced a smile. "You'd be surprised."

"Hmm. Well, we're behind right now." He handed me a box that weighed at least fifty pounds. I grunted, trying my best to manage the weight. "Take this over to the table and grab a clipboard with the list of items that should be inside. Once you check off all the items, label the box and place it on that pallet by the edge of our section."

I carefully exited the truck, scooting down the ramp with a little shuffle of my feet. I heaved the box onto the metal table next to Ivan and grabbed a clipboard that sat atop a wooden crate. With a box cutter, I popped open the box, which was filled with hundreds of the same packaged products. They looked like cheap in-ear headphones you could get for five bucks at the dollar store. I didn't think they were necessarily counterfeit. Then again, I should have expected I wouldn't stumble across the illegal stuff on day one.

I sifted through each package to make sure everything was in good shape. After marking them down on the inventory sheet, I resealed the brown box and placed a label on it. I hauled it onto the pallet JC directed me to earlier. When unloading the next box from the truck, my knees nearly buckled from the weight. Ivan rushed over to assist me, grabbing the box and helping me toward the table.

"You all right?" he asked.

"I didn't grip it as well as I thought," I said, rubbing my right wrist. "Thanks for the help."

"No problem. I was a newbie once too. Only, I didn't have anyone to help me."

"You kept your job though, so you must have done well."

"I don't know if that's a good thing." He chuckled softly as his narrow eyes crinkled at the corners. He opened his box of goods and said, "I've been trying to get out of here for a while now, but no one else is hiring. At least nothing that fits my qualifications."

I slid the box cutter through the tape of my next box as I asked, "How long have you been here?"

"Five years now."

"Wow, so you know the ins and outs of this place?"

"Not really. I keep my head down, do my work, and go home. Haven't even met the person who runs this joint."

I paused mid-cut, tilting my head. "Ted doesn't run it?"

"No, he's just the manager of this sector. There are about a dozen warehouses and loading docks in this area alone. The person who runs everything is nicknamed Red. Never met him, but I heard from those who have. They say he's a force to be reckoned with."

"Is that so?"

"Yup. If I were you, I'd get to work before you have to deal with him."

"Thanks for the heads up."

The two of us returned to our boxes, slaving away in the hot loading dock for the rest of our shift as this new information replayed in my mind.

At the end of my exhausting first day, I trudged through the apartment door, my feet and arms feeling like they were on fire. Natalie frowned at me, opening her arms on the couch. "Come here, you poor thing."

I dropped next to her, leaning into her soft embrace. "This day has been awful."

"Was it that bad?"

"I've never lifted so many heavy items in my life. Up and down the platform, sweating over large boxes crammed with hundreds of products. It was taxing, to say the least."

"Did you find out any information, at least?"

"Not a thing." I shook my head with a sad pout. "There were a few employees with the same tattoos that the gang wears, but that was about it. There might have been more of them with tattoos, just not in my line of sight."

"Anything else?"

"There's this super sweet guy named Ivan who helped me out and told me a few helpful snippets."

She leaned closer, a cheeky smirk on her face. "Is he hot?"

"Natalie. . . Please," I groaned.

"Oh, come on. It'll make work a lot more fun."

"It would be distracting. Plus, I want to gain his trust, not get into a relationship."

"If you say so." She leaned back on the couch. "So, what information did he give you?"

"The nickname of the head of the whole operation. This person could be completely unaffiliated with the gang and just manages the warehouse company under the owner, but I have to take everything I learn into account."

"What's their name? Is it, like, Killer or The Big MC?"

"It's not that obvious. It's just Red."

"Red?" She stroked her chin in thought. "That's interesting.

Maybe they are just a harmless person who runs the company, like you mentioned."

I massaged a sore shoulder, thinking about what I'd learned so far. "Well, I've only been there for a day. I'm sure I can gather more information over the rest of the week."

"What are you going to do now?"

"Take some aspirin and draw up some sketches of a few people I've met today. I'll probably shoot a detailed message over to the captain as well," I said, dragging myself off the couch, hunching over in the process.

Natalie stifled her laughter as I took each painful step to my room. "Good luck. I hope you feel better by tomorrow, because you're going to be doing it all over again."

"Ugh, don't remind me."

Once I hobbled into my bedroom, the first thing I did was down two aspirin, chasing it with water from my stainless-steel water bottle. All I wanted to do was crawl into bed to let my body relax, but I knew duty had to come first.

I started with the email to MDPD since that seemed to take precedence over the sketches. I was sure the captain and everyone else working this case wanted an update, even if it was minuscule. I typed up a brief message that explained my findings of the day and some of the people I deemed suspicious, including the manager. I also let the team know I'd be creating sketches by the end of the week so they could start diving into their identities.

After sending the email off to the captain, I shuffled over to my art table and started working on the outlines of my sketches. With a few lines here and there, labeling the back of each paper with what little information I'd gathered on each person, I started to feel inspired to flesh out the sketches. I wound up working late into the night to capture everything I could remember from that day.

Chapter 9

My alarm rang from across the room, jolting me awake. Still hunched over my art table, I lifted my head, a few paper notes stuck to my face. I plucked each one off before staggering to my nightstand to switch off the alarm. Checking the time, I decided it was late enough in the morning to start getting ready for another day at the warehouse. I had a quick breakfast and then dashed off to work.

When I got down to the docks, I strolled past the food trucks again. This time, there was a taco truck in place of the BBQ one. I wondered whether they rotated one of the trucks every day. As I checked out the taco truck, a familiar face caught my eye. Backtracking, I looked through the ordering window and found Bryan and Marco arguing in a hushed whisper.

"Um, guys," I said, trying to get their attention.

"Hey there," my brother said, leaning on the window counter. "Would you like some nachos?"

"I want to know what you two are doing here. And why are you running a taco truck?"

"We thought we'd give you a hand while you're undercover."

Marco chimed in, leaning next to my brother. "We didn't decide anything. *He* did. He sprung this on me when I walked into the station this morning."

Bryan shrugged and replied, "You're the one who suggested a taco truck."

"You said the only truck you could get a hold of was an ice-cream truck. That would have stood out like an igloo in Death Valley."

"It's Florida, and it's hot. Who wouldn't want ice cream?"

"Manly men who work at a loading dock," he quipped before adding in a hushed whisper, "who are also a part of a gang."

"Doesn't mean they wouldn't mind a popsicle every once in a while. I know I wouldn't."

"Of course you wouldn't," Marco sneered.

I tapped the bell they had placed at the ordering station. "Both of you, focus please."

Marco crossed his arms, making me notice just how toned his biceps were since he was only wearing a white tank top. "If anything goes wrong in there, don't hesitate to come and find us."

"You can also shoot me a text," Bryan tossed out.

"I'll do that." Just as I was about to turn around and head to work, I asked, "What's with the getup, though?"

Bryan looked down at his turquoise button-down shirt that

was adorned with a pattern of mini tacos. "What's wrong with our outfits?"

"Nothing with his, but yours is. . ."

Marco let out a stifled snort. "The worst part is, he already had that shirt in his locker."

Bryan glowered at his partner. "You never know when you need a party shirt ready to go."

"That's your go-to party shirt? No wonder you're still single."

"Coming from the guy who's also single."

"I choose to be. You, on the other hand," Marco said, raising an eyebrow.

I laughed at their bickering, until I noticed the time on my brother's watch. "You two duke it out while I get to work. I'm already running late."

"Wait!" my brother called. "Take these nachos so it doesn't look suspicious."

He slid over a basket of nachos that looked burnt, slathered in sour cream with crusty cheese underneath, and meat that didn't look like meat. I cringed as I tried to lift a chip that barely budged from its confinements. "Who made this?"

My brother gave me a proud grin. "Me, of course."

"I'm not eating this. I'll die."

Marco chimed in, "If you're lucky."

Bryan's grin dropped. "Guys, I can cook."

I took the nachos and said, "Maybe leave the cooking to Marco."

"Why, because he's Hispanic?"

"No, because I've seen your cooking skills. I'm sure anyone can make a meal better than you can."

Before Bryan could get another word in, I headed toward

the entrance to the loading dock. Ivan happened to be out front, smoking a cigarette when I reached the door. His lips curled into a smirk, his cigarette hanging from his mouth. "You actually showed up for day two."

"Do they usually bail?" I asked him.

"A good chunk."

"Well, I'm here to prove myself."

"Good to hear." He threw the butt on the ground before stomping it out. Ivan eyed the nachos in my hand and asked, "What the heck is that? They look like crap."

"I wanted to grab a quick bite for breakfast and stopped at the taco truck." I looked down at the nachos. Somehow, they looked worse than before. "I'm starting to think that was a bad call."

"I think I'll pass on that new truck, then. Was looking forward to it too."

"Well, maybe the other items on their menu are better than these."

He grimaced, still eyeing the depressing nachos. "I wouldn't risk it."

Breaking into laughter, we made our way inside the facility to get started on another strenuous day.

During the last break of the day, I lingered by the vending machines in the back of the warehouse. I decided to get a drink, but a hand stopped me from putting a dollar in the machine. Ivan stood next to me with his hand pressed against the money slot. "I wouldn't do that if I were you."

"Why?" I asked.

"This machine is notorious for taking money and not giving you anything back for it. And the times that it does give you what you asked for, the drinks taste flat."

"Even the water?"

"Maybe not flat, but a little weird."

I shot him a genuine smile. "Thanks for the heads up."

"If you ever want a drink or a snack, check the food vendors. They're better than what you'll get out of these things."

"I'll keep that in mind next time."

Ivan leaned against the busted vending machine, crossing his arms. "Can I ask you a question?"

I lifted an eyebrow. "It depends on what it is."

"Why did you take this job?"

"I lost my last job," I murmured. It wasn't a total lie, but I clearly couldn't tell him the truth.

"Gotcha. May I ask what the job was?"

"Well, you kind of did, but I don't mind answering. I was a freelance artist working for an older woman."

"Oh, I wouldn't have pictured you as a creative."

I narrowed my eyes playfully. "Is that a good thing or a bad thing?"

A soft chuckle left his chapped lips. "I'll get back to you on that."

I joined him in leaning against the vending machine. "I've been drawing since I can remember. I feel like that's the only thing I really know how to do," I said, feeling guilty since it wasn't what I was doing now.

"You know, I felt the same way with cooking."

"You can cook?"

"Don't let this face fool you. I can cook some mean dishes."

"That's awesome. How come you didn't become a chef?"

"Didn't think about it really. Most places want a college degree anyway, which I definitely don't have the funds to get."

"Maybe one day you'll be able to."

"Maybe." Ivan glanced at his watch. "We should get back to it. Our break is about up."

"At least there are only a couple more hours to go," I said as I walked with him to our workstation.

"Yep." He started to unpack the box he was working on. "Hey, if you ever want to come over to my apartment sometime, I can cook you something."

"Oh, that's a sweet offer. I'll think about it."

"Okay. . . I didn't mean to imply a date or anything. Just, like, work friends hanging out."

I held back a smile. "Right. I didn't think of it any other way."

For the rest of our shift, we worked in a comfortable silence as we skimmed through our boxes.

I was in the parking garage, trudging toward my scooter when I heard the screech of a vehicle pulling up beside me. Before I could get a good look at the black van, someone grabbed my arm and shoved me into the back. I started to struggle, ready to run, but when I cracked an eye open to look at my kidnapper, it was just Bryan and Marco. Releasing a long breath, I glared at the two. "Are you nuts?"

"We wanted to talk to you, and we didn't want to draw suspicion," Bryan answered.

"So, you threw me into a van?" I surveyed the confined

space, which featured gray walls and two benches on either side. "Where'd you get this thing anyway? The same place you got the food truck?"

Marco was the one who replied this time. "No, we got the food truck from a friend of mine. This is a police-issued vehicle that we use for stings and undercover operations."

"What do you guys want? I'd like to go home and get some rest."

"Any information you can give us?"

"Not really. I've only been there for two days and met a handful of people."

Bryan sighed and pressed, "You haven't observed any suspicious activity?"

"The only criminal-like thing that I've witnessed is littering and the processing of cheap products."

"Nothing else?"

"Not a thing. But I'm sure they're not going to keep their illegal activities in plain sight."

Marco grunted. "Of course they aren't. That's why we hired you to do some digging. Not to fraternize with your new colleagues."

"I'm not fraternizing with anybody."

"Marco has a point. You did seem kind of chummy with this guy." Bryan took out his phone and showed me a photo of Ivan and me from this morning.

I looked over the picture, my mouth agape. "You took a photo of us?"

"That's what we do, Cal. It's called surveillance and collecting evidence."

"Well, Ivan is a good guy. He's been nothing but helpful, and he doesn't have a tattoo."

"Are you sure about that?"

"I am. He just seems to keep to himself."

Marco pulled a tablet from under the bench he and Bryan were sitting on. He tapped away at the screen, pulling something up. "Ivan Carrano. He's thirty years old and currently lives in Dade County. Has a record that spans petty theft to grand theft, and even assault and battery."

Bryan's eyes bored into mine. "Still think he's a good guy?"

I shrugged. "He had a troubled past. So what? I'm sure he regrets his mistakes."

"For your sake, I hope so. I want you to stay safe, Cal. Don't let your guard down, whether they seem nice or not."

"I'll keep an eye on him, on *everyone* in that warehouse. But I'd like to think I'm good at reading people. And Ivan, he's not as bad as you think."

"Whatever you say. Just be smart about this, and don't let your feelings get in the way of your job."

"I won't."

Marco opened the back of the van, doing a quick scan of the area before looking back at me. "We'll see you tomorrow. And keep sending those check-ins to the captain. He likes being in the loop. We'll be giving him our brief later today."

"I'll do that when I get home," I said as I hopped out of the vehicle.

Marco gave a tight nod, and Bryan waved before the door closed behind me. Once they drove off, I shuffled toward my scooter, thoughtful. Maybe Ivan wasn't as clean as I'd first thought, but just because he had a few charges against him didn't mean he was all bad. Right?

Chapter 10

As my first week was coming to a close, I woke up to a dreary day outside. The clouds were a murky gray, and a few sprinkles of rain fell from the sky. Having lived in Florida my whole life, I was used to the rainy days. Even though I'd rather be curled up in bed, I had a job to do. I made my way to the warehouse, giving a quick sign of acknowledgement to Bryan and Marco who were stationed at the taco truck.

When I got into the warehouse, I found Ivan working diligently at our station. I was a bit wary of him now that I knew his past crimes, but there was still a part of me that believed he wasn't involved in the gang. As I reached our station, I noticed Ivan's worried expression. Actually, most people looked anxious as they scurried around the enormous warehouse with lifts, boxes, and products in hand. I sidled up next to Ivan. "What's going on? What's wrong with everyone?"

"We just got word that Red is coming in. It's a pretty big deal," Ivan mentioned as he continued his duties.

"He's never visited before, right?"

"Nope, never. This will be the first time most of us have seen Red in person. And I'd like to get on the boss's good side."

"I guess I should get to work, then."

"I would. Who knows when Red will pop in?"

I grabbed my tools and started to work hard until this mystery boss showed up.

After a few hours, Ted entered the room, and everyone went quiet. He marched to the center of the warehouse floor, lifted his hands, and bellowed, "Everyone, listen up. I just got word that Red will be here any minute. I want everyone on their best behavior. So, back to work."

We did as we were told. Within a few minutes, one of the garage doors lifted at the front end of the loading dock. A person walked in, flanked by two men in suits. When I finally caught a glimpse of the person known only as Red, my mouth nearly dropped to the floor. I'd been expecting a hulking man with mafia boss vibes to walk in. Not a tall, slender woman with long, wavy hair that was red as fire. Her licorice-black heels clacked against the cement floor as she lifted her dark shades to the top of her head. She stopped halfway through the facility, scrutinizing every inch of the place with narrowed eyes.

I tried to keep my head down, tinkering with a package that held a plush toy resembling a teddy bear. Thankfully, she didn't look for long before making her way toward the manager's office. Within seconds, Red vanished behind the door along with her two bodyguards. I turned to Ivan, whose visible bewilderment echoed my own.

"The guys I talked to always made Red out to be this tough, macho dude who didn't take any crap. I never thought it was a woman," Ivan said, shaking his head.

The door opened with a whoosh, and our eyes snapped back up to the office. Red strutted out with her hands on her hips. She scanned the place once more as her right foot tapped the floor. She turned to the nearest station and walked over to a man whose name I hadn't learned. He was quite buff, with a tattooed sleeve up his left arm. When she entered his line of sight, he stiffened and stood straight as a rod.

Red lifted the product he was reviewing and threw it to the ground. The only sound that could be heard was the echo of shattered merchandise pieces. She still didn't say a word as she continued to stare at him. She lifted her right hand and beckoned him over with a slim finger, its long acrylic nail painted as red as her hair. He glanced between her and her guards, who still hung close at either side of her. The man stumbled around his worktable, and she sauntered up next to him. I stood about six feet away, but I could still see the sweat dripping down his temple.

Like a viper, Red's hand shot up to the back of the guy's head, securing a vice-like grip on his thin blonde hair. The man hollered as she dragged him closer to her, maintaining her hold. She whispered something into his ear, her dark-purple lips accentuating every word. The guy tried to nod, but her grasp clearly made it difficult. Red released her hold before shoving the off-balanced man toward one of her guards. The guard towed him outside, while the other stayed close to Red.

"Nathan will no longer be working here," Red stated calmly as she dusted her hands together. "Let him be an example to all of you. Do not cross me or ignore the procedures we have set for this place. Here at Conwell's Oceanic Shipping Company, we pride ourselves on being number one in Miami and keeping ourselves out of trouble. When an employee of mine decides to chat with a competitor, slack off, or create delays, that makes me unhappy, especially if it affects the company as a whole. If you break my rules and I find out who you are, you'll be terminated immediately. Do I make myself clear?"

Everyone mumbled something under their breath, their heads bobbing slowly. Her lips spread into a sinister grin that showcased her pearly-white teeth. "I'm glad to hear it. Now, there is one more thing I want to discuss. I've heard from a little birdy that some illegal activities were traced back to us, and that is not okay. I do not want me, or my company's name, to be associated with anything of that nature. If the police are involved, as they say, then that will leave our company in shambles. Get your act together before I have to do more in-house cleaning. Do I make myself clear?"

The whole place grumbled out another string of words as we did a few seconds ago to show her that we understood.

"You may get to work."

Without missing a beat, everyone went back to their tasks, hustling to-and-fro as they grabbed boxes or lifted shipments with pallet trucks. I felt eyes burning into me. When I glanced up, I found Red staring me down. Was she suspicious of me because I was the newest employee at this warehouse? It must have been blatantly obvious. She strode over to me, her long legs clad in tight gray jeans. She crossed her arms in front of her chest and said, "You're the new recruit?"

"That's right," I replied as I halted my work.

"It's nice to see more women in this sector of the company."

"There aren't many of us here?"

"Only a handful the last time I checked." Red dug into the pocket of her black leather jacket, pulling out a cherry-red business card with white lettering. "If you're ever thinking about another position in this company, a higher one so to speak, maybe we can work something out."

She slid the card toward me on the table, and I looked it over. It wasn't anything fancy, just her nickname in an elegant cursive font, along with a couple of phone numbers and an email.

"I'll consider it," I said as I tucked it into my pocket.

"I'll be looking forward to your call," she said before spinning on her heel toward the entrance.

Once she was gone, a collective sigh could be heard throughout the warehouse. Soon, the hustle and bustle kicked up to its normal pace, and the loud racket of machinery drowned out the silence.

"Did she just offer you a job?" Ivan asked as he edged over to me.

"In a way, I think she did. . . which is quite odd, honestly," I mused, thinking about the card in my pocket.

"Are you going to take it?"

"I don't know what the position entails, so more than likely, I won't."

"It could be a good opportunity, though. I bet it has better pay and is less demanding than a job like this."

"Possibly, but I don't know if I have the qualifications for it."

"It's worth a shot. I'm sure she doesn't hand out opportunities like that to just anyone," he explained before going back to work.

I slipped the card back out of my pocket, looking it over once more. I knew I had to run this by the captain, along with Marco and Bryan, but this job offer seemed like it could steer our undercover investigation in the right direction.

Chapter 11

The office chair in the brief room swiveled as I wiggled my foot back and forth. The three men in the room chatted away, and I started to doze off. I hadn't gotten much sleep lately, too busy putting together the last of my sketches and writing out my observations. It didn't help that the laborious job I'd been muscling through had been draining my energy and making my body feel as if it were about to fall apart. Even the two doses of acetaminophen I took every day weren't strong enough to make the aches subside so I could relax.

Before I could fall into a deep slumber, Captain Baker directed a question toward me. "Callie, is that the file of the sketches you've done so far?"

Blinking my eyes open and clearing my throat, I nodded as I passed the manila folder to him. "Yes, it is. I drew about two dozen people from the warehouse. Most of the workers I drew are the ones who seemed suspicious. The top half are the ones who had a visible tattoo for Lucifer's Losers."

Captain Baker started spreading out the drawings on the table. Marco and Bryan took a few, studying my detailed sketches. The captain reached the end of my folder and found the layout designs I'd started of the warehouse. He unfolded the large paper and laid it out on the table. "You've created a layout of the place?"

"Kind of." I forced myself up from my chair, walking over to where he was standing. "I drew everything I've seen so far, or most of it. There's still plenty of the docks and warehouse that are a mystery."

"At least it's something. If we ever need to go in after-hours or get a warrant, we'll have the place mapped out."

"I'll finish this half up and get it photocopied for you."

"That would be great. It'll help us set up a plan in the future."

Marco leaned back in his chair. "These are all great, and I'm sure we'll be able to match some of these faces to mugshots. But this isn't going to get us any closer to what we're there for."

I crossed my arms, giving a small shrug. "I'm doing the best I can. I've only been there a week."

Bryan nodded and piped in, "You're doing great, Callie. We were just hoping for more information, but as you said, it's only been a week. It takes months to solve complicated cases like this one, sometimes even years. We're lucky to have anything at all with you volunteering to do this."

"I do have one more thing." I took out the business card Red had given me yesterday, sliding it toward my brother. "The owner of the place calls herself Red. She gave that to me, hoping I'd take her up on an offer for another position in her business."

He carefully picked it up by the edges and turned it from front to back. "What type of position?"

"No idea. She didn't tell me."

Marco stood from his chair, scanning the papers spread around the table. "Is she in one of these sketches?"

I dug through the drawings until I found the one depicting the intimidating woman. I lifted it, showing it to the men in the room. "This is her. It's a rough sketch since I just met her on Friday."

"Did you notice a tattoo?" Marco asked, grabbing the sketch from me.

"No. But the way she treated the man she fired was pretty aggressive. I wouldn't doubt that she's at least somewhat involved in the gang."

"Take the job," Marco said

"What now?"

"Take the job."

Bryan cut in, shaking his head. "No way. She's already in deeper than I'd like. She's not going to climb the ranks, getting closer to a gang leader just so we can bust these criminals."

Captain Baker cleared his throat, drawing our eyes to him. "Detective Dane, I must say Detective Suárez has a point. Having Callie in the upper sector of this company could get us closer to our goal."

Bryan slammed both hands on the table, holding his lean frame up. The vein on his neck bulging. "What if they know there is a bug in the system, and they're trying to eliminate it? That bug is my little sister. I don't want her getting any more involved than she already is."

I turned to my brother. "They are aware that someone is working with the police. They just don't know who."

"See, Captain? They are already onto us." Bryan waved his hands in front of him, a deep grimace carved into his face. "I think we should pull the plug on this idea and get my sister out of there."

Marco groaned. "We can't do that, Bryan. That'll be even more suspicious and make them want to hunt her down just like they did Wendy."

"He's right, Detective," Captain Baker explained. "This woman already has eyes on Callie. We can't risk it."

Bryan let out a huff as he slumped into his seat. "She should have never agreed to this."

I lifted my hand meekly and said, "I'm still here, and I feel like I should have a say in all of this."

Captain Baker nodded. "Of course. What do you want to do, Callie?"

"As much as I'd love to run away like my brother suggested, I know I can't do that." I placed my hands on my hips, letting out a breath through my parted lips as I weighed my choices. "Taking this job with Red could be our best bet, especially if she really is the head of Lucifer's Losers. Although if that's the case, I don't know how I'll avoid being found out and caught. I'm not that great of a liar."

"You have time to mull this over. I'm sure this Red woman wasn't expecting an answer right away, and it'll be less suspicious if you take your time in answering her. You can still collect information while you're undercover at the warehouse."

Marco started gathering some of the artwork from the table and said, "While you do that, we'll start reviewing everything we have so far and see if we can make any arrests. We can also scan that business card for prints and see if we get a hit on this woman."

As everyone dispersed, Bryan pulled me aside. "I'm sorry I got you into this, Cal."

I squeezed my brother's shoulder, shaking my head. "I chose to take on all of this. I needed a job, and you found me one. I could have easily turned it down, but I didn't. I wanted the stability. Maybe getting involved in this undercover sting was a bit audacious, but I did it, and I want to see it through."

"Just stay low, and don't give anyone reason to believe you're not who you say you are."

"What about Red? Should I take her up on her offer?"

"I have no idea. Just do what feels right to you, whether it benefits the case or not. Your life is the only thing I'm worried about."

"I'll run it by Natalie to see what she thinks. She seems to have good intuition when it comes to things like this."

"Whatever helps you decide." He planted a kiss on top of my head. "I have to help Marco. Call me or text me if you want to run it by me again."

"Will do."

After grabbing the leftover sketches and files, I followed him out of the briefing room. Each of us went our separate ways, him going to find Marco, and me heading home. It felt like every week I was left with a new decision to make, each one bigger than the last. Hopefully, this would be the last, for a little while at least.

I arrived at my apartment complex by mid-afternoon. The

meeting had run longer than I had anticipated, but I did feel like we'd gotten a little further in this stagnant case. When I reached the front door of my apartment, my hand hovered over the gold-colored knob. The door was ajar, which was unusual. I pushed it open with my fingertips, and the scene that greeted me made my hair stand on end.

The place looked as if a tornado had torn through it. Wading through the wreck that remained, I managed to get to my room, where the same scene repeated itself. Everything was strewn about. The furniture was turned practically upside down, and my drawers were pulled out of the dressers. I scurried over to Natalie's room, where even her space was in shambles.

I heard the door open. "Whoa, what happened in here?" came Natalie's voice.

I walked back out to the living room and said, "That's what I would like to know, but from the looks of it, we've been ransacked."

"Were we robbed?"

"I'm not sure. It's hard to tell if anything is missing in this mess."

"You don't think this has anything to do with your current job, do you?"

"I have a feeling it does," I stated as I pulled out my phone and started dialing Bryan's number.

"Are you calling the cops?" Natalie asked, beginning to dig through the mess on the floor.

"Close. My brother."

Bryan answered quickly, and his concerned voice echoed through the receiver. "What's wrong?"

"There's a bit of a situation at my apartment. Someone

broke in and tore our place apart," I replied.

"Damn. . . Stay put, and don't touch anything. Marco and I will be right over with a squad of uniformed officers, okay?"

"Got it. I'll see you soon."

Hanging up, I placed the phone back into my pants pocket. Natalie leaned against the kitchen counter and asked, "Is your brother coming over?"

"Yep, along with some uniformed cops and his partner."

"Think I should put something sexier on? Men in uniform are just my type."

"Every man is your type," I said with a chuckle. "But he said to not touch anything, so I wouldn't risk digging for your sexy clothes."

"Too bad. . . Think they'll care about that pile I moved?"

I glanced down at the mess of items. "Eh, I'm sure it's fine."

Ten minutes later, Bryan showed up with Marco and the squad in tow. They blocked off our front door with crime scene tape and started rummaging through our untidy apartment. As they conducted their investigation, lifting prints and sifting through stuff for evidence, Bryan and Marco interviewed me and Natalie. Marco was jotting our answers on a miniature notepad as he asked, "Who found the apartment like this first?"

I raised my hand. "That would be me. The door was ajar when I got back from our meeting at the precinct."

"There was no one here when you arrived?"

"No. The place was empty."

Bryan nodded and asked Natalie, "How about you, Natalie? Did you notice anything suspicious before you left or when you got back?"

Natalie shrugged her right shoulder and shook her head. "No, nothing. I mean, this neighborhood is kind of shady to begin with, so I don't think I would have noticed someone or something out of place."

"Is anything missing?"

"It's kind of a disaster in here. There's no way of telling."

"How about you, Cal? Do you notice anything missing?"

I looked around at our pigsty of a living room and replied, "I can't tell."

Marco closed his notebook, tucking it in the pocket of his gray blazer. "At least neither of you were home during this incident. It could have ended much worse."

"Do you think this has something to do with the case?"

"This doesn't seem like a typical burglary. My best guess is that this does indeed have something to do with the case."

"Am I in danger? Or Natalie?"

Bryan pursed his lips, breathing out a sigh before he answered me. "There's a possibility. We don't know whether they're aware of your true identity. If you've been compromised, then you could be in grave danger. You and anyone around you. If they're just checking employees out because they know there's a rat in the mix, then you could be safe."

"In other words, you have no idea, and we're walking on eggshells."

"Basically."

I smoothed back the short curls on top of my head as I thought about the predicament I had put myself in. "This is too much. I shouldn't have gone through with this— any of this. I should have just gone with the teaching job."

To my surprise, Marco was the one to acknowledge my concerns. "Don't wimp out now. We've come too far to start backtracking. You'll go in on Monday, pretending everything is A-okay, and you won't give those people any reason to believe that the outsider is you. I know you don't want to let Wendy or Josephine down, so try to pull yourself together and see this through."

Bryan grunted, casting his partner a serious glare. "She should be out of this. There is too much at stake. We're talking about people's lives."

"It's too late for that now. We have to keep going, or there'll be even more problems. You know that, Detective Dane."

"Then what do we do now?"

"We continue our investigation. Arrest those that we can and let Callie finish what she was chosen to do."

He huffed, his nostrils flaring. "Fine. I'll meet you back at the precinct after I take Callie and Natalie somewhere safe."

Marco gave us a short nod of approval before leaving the apartment. I eyed my brother, who looked to be in deep thought as his eyebrows knitted together. "Where are you going to take us?"

"Our parents' house."

"Did we have to come here?" I grumbled to my brother as Natalie and I pulled our small duffel bags out of his trunk.

Bryan closed his trunk, turning to me. "It's the safest place on such short notice. A rich and gated neighborhood with twenty-four-hour surveillance? You can't beat that."

Natalie butted in, "It'll be fun. Plus, I like your parents and their swanky tub."

I groaned as we made our way up the front steps. "I can't deal with them for more than a couple of days."

Bryan smiled as he rang the doorbell. "Hopefully, this case won't take much longer. Just hang in there, okay?"

"All right, but I'm not going to like it."

"I wasn't planning on it."

The door opened, revealing my father with a giant grin on his face. He pulled me into a massive hug, like always, but I could tell he was worried. It felt a bit stronger than his usual embrace. "I'm glad you're okay, snuggle bug."

I patted his back. "Me too."

"Nice to see you again, Natalie," my father said, giving her a courteous wave.

Natalie smiled. "You too. Thanks for taking us in."

"Anything for my kids and their friends."

As he ushered us inside, I asked, "Is Mom here?"

"No, she had some errands to run. She'll be back soon, though."

Bryan clapped his hands together. "I'd love to stay, but I need to go back to the precinct. I'll be back later tonight to make sure everyone is okay. But don't hesitate to call if anything goes wrong."

My dad hugged him and whispered, just loud enough for me to hear, "Take care of yourself."

"I will."

Bryan said his goodbyes and then left our parents' home. My dad took our bags from us, making his way up the marble staircase. "Come on, you two. I set up the guest bedroom for Natalie, and your room hasn't been touched since you moved out, Cal."

As we followed him, I said, "Thank you. I'll contribute to any extra expenses that might come up from us being here."

"Nonsense," he said as he dropped our bags at our respective rooms. "All we want to do is keep you safe. You don't owe us a thing."

"I hope we don't have to stay for long," I said, my shoulders sinking.

Dad gave me an affectionate look. "Me neither, but only because what you're involved in is terrifying, and I don't want anything happening to you."

"I know. I just hope I can help them solve this case."

He pulled me into his side, planting a gentle kiss on my forehead. "You will. You're the bravest and strongest woman I know, besides your mother. You can do this."

"I hate to interrupt, but I'm starving. What are we having for dinner? Mr. Dane's famous chili I hope," Natalie said as she leaned against the doorframe of the guest bedroom.

My father let out a hearty chuckle. "I can whip up a quick batch of my chili. I'll let you two get settled, then."

He headed back downstairs, and I hauled my duffel bag into my high-school bedroom. I plopped the bag onto my bed and looked around. My room was still cluttered with art supplies, a corkboard crammed with photographs, and a few collectible figures I had forgotten about. I sat at my old desk, looking over the forgotten half-finished sketches I had started during high school. Natalie joined me in my room and glanced around the quaint space. "You know, I don't think I've ever seen your room when we've come over to visit."

"There isn't much to see. Just a normal teenage girl's room," I said, gesturing around the place.

"I guess so. It's kind of cute, though." She sat on my bed,

running her hand over the cheap floral-print blanket I had draped over the comforter. "Do you think you'll figure this out?"

"I sure hope so. You see these kinds of crazy scenarios on television shows and movies, ordinary people solving crimes. But it's so much different being in the heart of it. It's not as easy as it looks."

Natalie was quiet for a moment. "What's next?"

"I have to figure out whether I'm taking this job offer from the owner who calls herself Red. It might aid the investigation, but it could lead to even more chaos."

Natalie shrugged. "I say do it. What's the worst that can happen?"

"Death," I mumbled with a sigh. "That's the worst that can happen."

"It seems like that's already a possibility."

"You do have a point. No matter how I look at it, danger is right around the corner."

"So, you're going to take it?"

I pursed my lips in thought. "I think I am. Not right away, but soon."

"By the way, you didn't tell me your brother's partner was fine as heck," Natalie said, raising a brow as a smirk spread across her face.

"He's okay looking," I said.

"Just okay? He should have been a model instead of a detective."

"Why are we friends again?" I scoffed.

She walked over to me, squeezing my shoulders as she whispered in my ear, "Because I'm awesome."

"Sure." I stood up from the bed with a faint yawn. "I'm

going to take a quick shower. How about you?"

"I'm going to go see if your dad needs any help with the chili. Maybe I can grab a few bites before dinner."

I laughed as she practically skipped out of my room. With a sigh, I grabbed some clothes from my duffel and went to take my shower. Staying with my parents wasn't ideal, but at least it was something. For now.

Chapter 12

The weekend flew by as I continued my back-and-forth pondering about whether to take up the offer from Red. When I stepped into the warehouse, I noticed that Ivan wasn't at our station. I looked around the large building, but I didn't see him anywhere. Making my way up to JC, I asked, "Do you know where Ivan is?"

"Out back, smoking like a chimney," J.C. stated as he loaded a box into the back trailer of a truck. "If you go talk to him, tell him he has two minutes to get in here before I report him to the manager."

"Thanks. I'll let him know."

I made my way toward the back door, heading out to the back lot, a place I'd never been before. I spotted a line of storage units with red metal doors occupying the lot. Hundreds of shipping containers were also scattered around the spacious dock, some stacked at least four containers high. Finding Ivan sitting on a black crate by some green dumpsters, I sauntered over to him. He looked stressed as he puffed on the cigarette that hung between his lips. The crow's-foot creases by his eyes seemed prominent as he stared out at the inlet.

"Are you okay, Ivan?" I asked.

He looked up at me, his eyes wide with what I presumed was fear. He stumbled to his feet, grabbing my arm and pulling me closer. He glanced around before whispering, "There's something strange going on around here."

"What do you mean?"

"I was asked to come into work yesterday, and I helped move a few pallets into some of those storage units back there. When I was putting in the last pallet, I could have sworn I heard a girl's voice calling out for help from one of the units nearby. I tried to find where it was coming from, but the person I was working with told me to move it along."

"Are you sure?"

"I'm positive!" One of the other workers wandering around the back lot looked over at us, and Ivan lowered his voice a few decibels. "They're holding people in here."

"You didn't know what they were doing here?" I asked, my head cocked to the side.

"No. . . I mean, I always suspected something, like drugs or counterfeit products, but not people."

I scanned our surroundings to make sure no one was listening in, like Ivan did earlier. I murmured in a low voice, "The gang who runs this shipping company are suspected of smuggling people. Possibly other things too."

"How do you. . .?" He went quiet for a split second. "You're the spy working with the feds. The one Red was talking about the other day."

"Shh, not so loud. I'm helping the MDPD with their case, but I'm not technically a cop. I'm just a forensic artist."

"If they find out, you're dead. You know that, right?"

"I'm aware. Just don't say anything, okay?"

"I won't." His eyes drifted down before locking back onto mine. "Are you any closer to putting an end to this gang?"

"Not really, but with the information you gave me just now, maybe we can get closer to tearing this whole operation down."

The back door to the warehouse swung open, and we wheeled around to see JC glaring from the top step. "You two aren't getting paid to chat to your hearts' content. Now get in here and help me with these packages."

Ivan threw his cigarette butt to the ground, stomping it out with a look of annoyance. "We'll be right there, JC"

Once JC was out of earshot, I whispered to Ivan, "So, you'll keep this between us?"

"Of course. I like you. And honestly, after what you just told me, I want to see this place burn, even if I do lose my job."

"Thank you, Ivan. This means a lot."

"Don't worry about it. Just be careful."

"I'll try."

Ivan started back up the steps into the warehouse, and I pulled out my phone to type up a quick message about what I'd just learned. I shot it over to Bryan and swiftly made my way back inside to get to work.

Once my shift ended, and I checked the text that Bryan had sent earlier in the day. He wanted to talk to me after work, so he'd stop by our parents' house later tonight. After returning to the house, I got cleaned up— I hated sitting around in hours' worth of sweat— and waited for him in our parents' den. I bounced my leg anxiously as I sat on the couch facing the rarely used fireplace. Every few minutes, I wound up checking my phone to see the time or check whether Bryan texted me.

"Cal, is it true? Did they find someone?" Bryan asked as he trudged into the room.

"They didn't find anyone. They just heard someone's voice coming from a storage unit," I replied.

"That's not going to help our case. A visual would be more concrete than hearing a noise that could have been nothing."

"At least it's a step in the right direction, right?"

"Who did you say provided this evidence?"

"Ivan, the guy I work with."

Bryan pinched the bridge of his nose as he shook his head. "He's not a credible source. He has a record, Cal. Even if we got him to testify against a major gang, he'd be hard for the jury to believe."

"Why would he lie about something like this?" I asked, my voice rising in frustration.

"To make sure that it doesn't come back to him if he's involved in any way."

"He looked scared, Bry. After seeing him like that, I don't think he's involved at all. He could help us."

"I know you like this guy, but you have to see this situation from every angle. Until we get solid evidence that there are indeed people being smuggled to and from that facility, we can't believe everything we hear."

"I don't 'like' him, at least in the way you're thinking. He's a friend, and I'm going to believe that he's innocent and telling the truth."

"Does he know?"

"Know what?"

"About why you're really there?"

"I may have let it slip, but as I said, I trust him."

A look of shock cloaked his face. "Callie. . . If he tells anyone your identity, you're dead."

I threw my hands up. "He won't!"

"You don't know that!" Bryan yelled, pointing a stern finger at me. "And let's say he isn't involved, but they catch wind that he knows. I bet he won't hesitate to sing like a canary to save his own hide."

"No, you're wrong. He's a good guy. No matter what he might have done in his past, he wouldn't tell."

"For your sake, I hope you're right."

My mother sashayed into the room in her silk robe, her arms crossed. "My goodness, what is going on in here? Your father and I can hear you from upstairs."

"It's fine, Mother. I was just leaving," Bryan said with a sigh. "I hope you both have a good night."

He left the room, stomping toward the front door. My mother looked at me with a frown. "What did you do, Callie?"

I scoffed, rolling my eyes. "Of course it's my fault."

"Your brother hardly ever gets that upset. You had to have done something."

"All I did was give him information that he doesn't want to believe because of his stupid police ideology. That's all."

"You know he's worried about you. We all are."

"You have a funny way of showing it," I mumbled as I brushed past her to head up to bed.

Before I could leave, my mother grabbed me and tugged me into a surprise hug. I stiffened in her grasp as I tried to comprehend what was happening. "I know I don't do this often. But I do care about you, Callie. You're my only daughter, and having you doing something so dangerous scares me. We may clash from time to time, but I love you, and I don't want to lose you."

I tried to hold back the tears that sprung to my eyes at her words. But after the last couple of months, it was hard. I let the tears flow out as I held my mother close, something I hadn't done in many years. "All I've ever wanted to do was make you proud. To show you that I can take care of myself."

"You do make me proud. It may not be what I wanted for you, but I am proud to see the things you can do."

"I'm scared, mom. What if I can't do this?"

"You can do this. I know you can. You just have to believe in yourself and believe that your brother is going to protect you if anything goes wrong."

"Do you wish you would have supported me before it came to this?"

Her hands slid toward my arms so she could pull away enough to look me in the eye. "I do. But it's too late for that now. Whatever you may choose in the future, I'm rooting for you."

I nodded as I wiped the tears away. "Thank you, Mom."

"Any time, Callie," she said as she quickly kissed my cheek. "Have a goodnight, sweetie."

I told her goodnight before she made her way up the stairs to bed. I turned off the lights to the den before I headed off to my own room. As I lay on my childhood bed, staring at the dark ceiling above, I reached toward the nightstand and grabbed a piece of paper where I'd copied Red's number. Maybe it was time to take her up on that offer and get down to the heart of this organization once and for all.

Chapter 13

I was feeling pumped after my conversations last night. Nothing was going to take me down from this high I was riding. Today, I was going to take a new approach to this undercover case. My peppy footsteps started to falter as I made my way to my station, noticing that yet again, Ivan wasn't there. This time. another guy was in his place, leaving me confused and worried. Grabbing the man's attention, I asked, "Where's Ivan?"

The muscular man shrugged his wide shoulders as he answered, "No clue. Ted called me up this morning and asked if I could work today."

JC hopped out of the truck with a package in his arms. I walked over to him. "JC, do you know where Ivan is?"

"Why would I know? I ain't his keeper," JC said as he placed the box on top of the metal table.

"I just thought you might have heard something."

"Nope, not a thing. I'm sure he'll be back tomorrow"

I swallowed down a lump in my throat. "I'm sure he will."

"Now get to work. I don't want to fall behind again."

I did as I was told, but I couldn't stop my mind from wandering off, thinking about where Ivan could be.

I asked Bryan if I could meet up with him and Marco at the precinct after work. He agreed to it, so that's where I was headed. I was still worried about Ivan, reflecting on about his random disappearance nonstop. It wouldn't have been unusual if he hadn't just divulged a trove of sensitive information to me yesterday. If the gang caught wind that he might know something and could hurt their business, they wouldn't hesitate to take him out. I was sure Bryan and Marco would have a different opinion when I spoke with them in a few minutes, but I didn't think Ivan's disappearance was a coincidence.

When I got to the precinct, Bryan and Marco were in the meeting room, engaged in conversation. Their chatter ended abruptly once I entered the room. Marco was the first to address me when I reached the head of the table. "Why did you call us here this evening? Did you get a break in the case?"

"Ivan is missing. He wasn't at work today," I told them.

"That's the news you wanted to share with us?"

"Yes. You two might not believe anything is wrong with his sudden disappearance, but I do."

Bryan sighed as he leaned forward to look at me. "Of course there could be something wrong, but it's barely been twenty-four hours since he went missing, right?"

"I guess that's about right."

"Haven't you ever taken a sick day from work?"

"Well, yeah. I'm pretty sure we've all had to at some point."

"Exactly. For all we know, Ivan decided to take the day off, and he's running personal errands."

I shook my head as I folded my arms over my chest. "I just don't think he'd do something like that, not after what we talked about yesterday."

Marco stood, picking up the iPad that was on the table in front of him. "Which gives me reasons to believe that he's still in on this. Whether you want to believe he's innocent or not."

I shot him a glare. "Ivan wouldn't do that."

"Okay, hypothetically speaking, let's say you're right about Ivan's intentions. If he is missing, and Lucifer's Losers got hold of him, who's to say he isn't going to tell them everything when they rough him up a little bit?"

"I don't think he'd give me up that easy. He's a strong guy. I'm sure he can handle anything they throw at him."

"People would do anything to stay alive," he replied, his expression unreadable.

Marco left the room before I could say anything more. Bryan came up to me, placing a caring hand on my upper arm. "Look, Cal. I know you care for this guy, but we can't go off of nothing. He'll turn up tomorrow, I promise."

I pushed his arm away, narrowing my eyes at him. "He's not going to be in tomorrow. I just wish you would take this seriously and look for him."

"We can't do that. He's not on our radar right now, so wherever he may be is not of our concern. If he's not in tomorrow, then we'll look into his whereabouts."

"Fine, whatever," I mumbled as I started for the exit. "If

you won't expand your search, I will."

I heard him call after me, asking what I was going to do, but I didn't turn back. I knew what my next move was, whether my brother and the precinct liked it or not.

Back at my parents' place, I jogged up to my room to make a phone call. I paced my old bedroom like an expecting father, clutching my phone as I stared at the number that I had typed in. Once I placed this phone call, there was no going back. But it was the only thing I could try to get to the bottom of this case. Plus, the faster I finished this, the faster I could put in my resignation letter. I didn't think I could handle working with the MDPD anymore. With my heart beating a mile a minute, I hovered my thumb over the green call button before I slowly pressed it. My heart raced faster as the phone started to ring. With a clammy and shaky hand, I lifted the device to my ear and waited for an answer.

"Conwell's Oceanic Shipping Company. How may I help you?" a female voice echoed cheerfully on the other end.

"Hi, my name is Callie Da—" I halted, clearing my throat before correcting, "My name is Callie Duncan, and I was told by Red to contact her."

"Hmm. . . I don't see you on our list, and we don't usually take unsolicited calls. But Ms. Red is in between meetings right now." I heard the girl shuffle around on the other end. "Give me one moment, please. I'll have to converse with Ms. Red before patching you through."

I couldn't even give her a response before an audible click sounded, and upbeat elevator music began playing through the speaker. As I waited on hold, I looked over the half-finished artwork I had made of Red, planning to finish it once I spoke with her again. That is, if she gave me the opportunity she offered me the other day.

The elevator music stopped abruptly, and the receptionist came back on. "Hello, Ms. Duncan. Ms. Red said I can patch you through. Have a good evening."

I opened my mouth to thank her, but the phone started ringing before I could get the words out. The phone barely finished its first ring before Red's honeyed voice filled my ear. "Ms. Duncan, I didn't think you'd give me a call. I'm quite surprised, but I'm happy you did. So, what spawned this late-night call?"

"I was thinking about that offer you mentioned the other day. I would like to take you up on it."

"Oh, my offer. It is still on the table if you're interested. I'm sure I could find you a spot in one of my offices."

"Yes, I'm interested."

"Okay then. I'll have a vehicle waiting for you outside of work when you come in for your shift tomorrow. Don't be late. If there is one thing I appreciate, it's punctuality."

"I understand. I'll be there first thing tomorrow morning."

"Great to hear that, Ms. Duncan. I'll see you tomorrow."

The line went dead, silence now filling my empty room. I tossed my phone aside before glancing at the small alarm clock at the side of my bed. It wasn't extremely late, but I wanted to be ready for my impromptu interview tomorrow. I wondered whether I should tell Bryan about what I'd done, but I decided against it. I could handle this on my own. If it did warrant a briefing after my visit, then I'd let the team know. For now, I'd keep this to myself. The precinct didn't seem to take me seriously anyway. I just hoped I wouldn't regret this.

Chapter 14

I arrived at the docks a few minutes earlier than usual. I didn't want to risk being late, either by getting stuck in Miami's early-morning traffic or having something come up while I was getting ready. As I made my way to the entrance of the loading docks, I made sure to scurry past the taco truck my brother and Marco were still running. I didn't want to be stopped and questioned as I went to conduct my own secretive undercover work. Thankfully, the two were distracted as I passed by. Both Marco and Bryan were bickering in the back of the truck. All their arguing made me wonder how they'd managed to work together for so long.

When I got to the entrance of the loading docks, I noticed a sleek black Escalade parked by the curb. A tall, bald man was leaning against the passenger-side door, his suit-clad arms crossed in front of him. His face was expressionless, though most of it was hidden behind his dark shades. I nervously walked up to the intimidating man and asked, "Are you here to pick up Callie Duncan?"

"Yeah, you her?" he asked in a low and monotonous voice.

"That's me."

He let out a short grunt as he lifted himself off of the door. He opened the back door of the vehicle, gesturing with his hand for me to get in. I didn't hesitate to follow his orders. He didn't seem like a fellow with a lot of patience. As I huddled on the leather seat in the spacious luxury vehicle, my left leg jittered up and down. I peered out the tinted window and fixed my eyes on my work building, wondering whether Ivan was actually here today or still MIA. I didn't expect my meeting with Red would run late, especially since it was early in the morning, so I'd be able to work the rest of my shift and see if Ivan was in.

As we zoomed through the city streets, weaving in and out of downtown traffic, I pulled out my phone. I quickly turned the ringer off so it wouldn't disturb me, or anyone I was with, during this undercover run. Before I could put it back in my pocket, a text message came through from Bryan. After checking to confirm that the driver was distracted by the road, I opened up the message to see what my brother wanted.

"*Who was that guy? Where'd you go?*" Bryan's text said.

I didn't want to leave him hanging, so I shot back a simple message to keep him from worrying. "*Later.*"

I was sure he wouldn't be happy with that response, but that was all I could say right now. I stuffed my phone back into my pants pocket and continued to gaze at the high-rises and palm trees that whizzed past the dark window. Soon, we were pulling up next to one of the many high-rises in the area, and the driver exited the vehicle. When he opened my door, I couldn't help but stare up at the tall building in front of me. The whole building was made up of glass paneling, making it shine in the bright morning sun.

"Take the elevator to the thirtieth floor. Once you're there, the receptionist will tell you what to do. I'll be waiting for you out here when you're done," my driver said.

"Thanks," I mumbled before heading into the office building.

I took the immaculate elevator to the thirtieth floor, as instructed, and found myself gawking at the luxurious place. For a business that seemed to be into some shady stuff, they sure knew how to keep a clean profile. The gray, marbled tiles glimmered as I stepped off the elevator. I could practically see myself in the perfectly shined tiles. On the center wall at the far end of the room, behind the reception desk, was a silver 3D sign of the company's name and logo. Several beige chairs were scattered around the lobby along with potted plants of all shapes and sizes. The view from this floor wasn't so bad either. It overlooked the city of Miami. Even the beach, albeit small, was still visible. Trying to gather myself mentally, I walked up to the receptionist, who raised a petite finger at me.

"Please hold," she said before tapping her headset. "Name?"

"Me?" I asked since she wasn't looking in my direction when she asked.

She shot me a quick glance and said, "Yes, you. Name?"

"Callie Duncan."

"You're early. Ms. Red is still in her phone conference. Have a seat, and I'll call you when she's ready."

I gave the woman a brief nod before taking a seat by one of

the large windows. As I sat there waiting, I started to get nervous about not having told Bryan and Marco my whereabouts. For all I knew, I could have been stepping into a trap. Then again, the two rarely took me seriously whenever I had an idea about the investigation. I just hoped they were smart enough to piece things together in case I didn't make it back to the loading docks.

"Callie Duncan. She'll see you now," the receptionist said from her desk.

I approached the desk again and asked, "Where is her office located?"

"Straight down the hall. The very last door is hers. Can't miss it," she replied, pointing toward the hallway with a dark-blue pen. "By the way, I'd lose that hat if I were you. She hates them in her office."

I had completely forgotten that I still had my work hat on. After yanking it off my head, I quickly fiddled with my short brown locks, hoping my hat hair wasn't an issue. The Florida humidity probably didn't help in the matter. Once I felt confident enough with myself, I made my way down the hall toward Red's office. On my way, I passed several workers, mostly women, bustling about the hall, gliding from one room to another. I wondered what types of jobs they did here besides the basics like accounting and filing.

When I reached Red's door, I wasn't surprised that it stood out from everyone else's. It was a dark red color, fitting her brand to a tee. It was slightly ajar, so I peeked in and gave a faint knock on the wood-paneled door. She didn't spare me a glance since her eyes were glued to her computer screen, but she still acknowledged my presence. "Come in, Callie, and close the door."

I eased the door shut before making my way into her office. It was just as nice as the lobby area, which wasn't much of a shock. I timidly sat on one of the velvet seats that were a deep shade of maroon, studying the red-headed woman in front of me. Wringing the cap in my hand, I waited for the woman to address me once more.

She twisted her body toward me, her black dress shirt fitting snug on her lean body. She flashed me a charming smile. "I'm glad you could make it, and on time too."

"I'd rather please the person who signs my checks than make them regret hiring me," I said casually.

"Smart move." She turned back to her computer, clicking away at the keyboard. "I see here in your file that you have decent credentials. It makes me wonder why you chose to seek employment as a warehouse worker."

"There weren't many job opportunities in Miami that fit my qualifications."

"Understandable. Jobs have been hard to come by over the last few years."

"They definitely have."

Red leaned closer to me, resting her folded arms on her uncluttered desk. "When a position opens up, I usually try to hire internally before I search for an external candidate. I feel it's better for everyone that way. We don't have many positions open at this time, at least in this sector of the company. But one of my employees will be leaving in a few months, and I thought I'd find her successor in the meantime."

"What's the job?" I asked.

"For now, social media intern. We had a few in the position over the last two years, but none stayed longer than seven months. With our social media manager leaving, we'd like to have another candidate to move up the ranks during these upcoming months."

"I'm guessing it's a paid internship?"

"Yes. It'll be around the same wage you're earning now, but the work will be less grueling, and in the comfort of an airconditioned office."

"That does sound tempting."

"I'm sure it does." Red flashed me a short smirk, reclining in her office chair. "On top of that, if you stay long enough and take over the management position, you'll be seeing a nice increase in your earnings."

I tried to act interested, hoping I looked believable. "I do like the sound of that. Is there a chance I can think on it, or is it a take-or-leave-it offer?"

"I can give you a week. There's no need for us to hire right away, but I wanted to sort out my possibilities now."

"A week is all I need."

"Then I'll hear from you in a week." Red's landline started to ring, interrupting our conversation. She stared down at the phone, giving it a menacing glare before raising a finger at me. "One second. I told them not to interrupt me during our meeting, but they never listen."

Her slim fingers picked up the phone with a bone-crunching grip, and she whispered coldly to the person on the other end, "What do you want? I am busy. . . You did, and you couldn't take care of it yourself. That isn't surprising news. . . We'll take care of it later. Call me in ten."

Red hung up the phone before turning back to me with a sympathetic smile. "I'm sorry about that. It wasn't as urgent as they thought, but it's still something I need to look into."

"It's fine. Thanks for having me in today," I said, forcing a smile.

"The pleasure was all mine. I'll talk to you next week." She reached her petite alabaster hand out for me to shake and said, "Good day, Ms. Duncan."

I shook her hand, the softness of her skin making me feel slightly self-conscious of my own. "Good day, Ms. Red."

I found my way out of the building with ease, meeting with the driver downstairs like he'd told me to earlier. The ride back seemed a lot shorter than the ride there, probably because most of the commuter traffic had died down since then. It barely gave me time to ponder Red's potential involvement in Lucifer's Losers. She may have been a little rough around the edges, but if you were running a business in an industry dominated by men, then you would have to be tough. She seemed genuine while I spoke with her today. My personal opinion was that she didn't know what was happening behind her back. Then again, I'd never realized my college boyfriend was running an illegal sports-betting ring in his dorm room. Needless to say, my track record wasn't the best when it came to profiling people. Did that mean I was wrong about Ivan, too?

After arriving back at the warehouse, I learned that he wasn't at work for today's shift either. There were only two possible scenarios that made sense in this new, mysterious missing-person case. Either he was in danger, or he was involved in these crimes we were trying to crack down on. I was still holding out hope that my first impression was right, and he was still trustworthy. I just hoped he was safe because I'd feel nothing but guilt if I got him killed.

When I rolled into my parents' driveway after my shift, I wasn't surprised to see Bryan and Marco waiting for me on the living-room couch. The two men stood when I entered the room, and I braced myself for the onslaught of questions. Of course, my brother was the first to spark the conversation about my early-morning whereabouts. "Where were you, Cal?"

"I had a meeting with Red, the head of Conwell's Oceanic Shipping Company," I said.

"The one who gave you the card? Why didn't you tell us that you were going to meet with her?"

I placed my hands on my hips. "It was something I wanted to do on my own."

"This is dangerous stuff. Anything could have happened while you were off trying to solve this case on your own, and we wouldn't have known where to look."

Marco stepped between us, trying to defuse our sibling quarrel. "Look, it doesn't matter now. She's safe, and we know where she was. Let's just get any information she gathered during her spontaneous meeting and call it a night."

Bryan grumbled something under his breath before letting out a sigh, nodding briefly. "You're right. Callie, can you tell us anything?"

I let out a short chuckle as I scratched awkwardly at the back of my neck. "This may not be what you wanted to hear, but I didn't get any bad vibes from Red while I was there. Everything seemed normal to me."

Bryan narrowed his eyes. "You're joking."

"No, I'm not. It seemed like a regular big business, looking to help their employees."

Marco crossed his arms and asked, "There's nothing else you may have noticed?"

"The only thing that stood out was the phone call she received. She seemed a little distressed and wanted the person on the other end to handle whatever the situation was."

"That could be anything."

"I'm aware."

Bryan huffed. "This case is going nowhere. Dead end after dead end."

"Agreed," Marco replied. "With the lack of information and evidence at every turn, we're not making a single dent in solving this thing. We may just have to tag it as a cold case."

"What?" I snapped, glancing between the two. "You're just going to give up?"

"We don't want to give up, but sometimes that's how it has to be. There are tens of thousands of cases in the cold-case database. Some eventually get solved, and some never do. That's just how it works."

"What about Ivan? He's still gone. . . What if he's the missing link or something?"

Bryan gave me a one-shoulder shrug. "He isn't our priority, but if we have the time, we'll see if we can come up with something. Maybe it can lead to more clues, but I'm not holding my breath."

"I know you don't believe that something's wrong with his disappearance, but I have this feeling that it ties into the case more than you think."

"It probably does, but there's still nothing concrete. We will try to look into it for you, Cal. I promise."

"Thank you, Bry."

With a brief hug and a quick goodbye, Bryan and Marco left

the house. I was still frustrated with the way they were treating Ivan's disappearance. He could be dying, and I'd feel guilty that I hadn't done everything in my power to help him. Checking the clock on my parents' mantel, I decided a late-night run was in order. I was sure Bryan and Marco wouldn't approve of what I was about to do, especially after the stunt I pulled this morning. But if they weren't going to take my concerns seriously, there was only one thing to do— take matters into my own hands.

Chapter 15

It was eerie being down at the loading docks after dark. The dimly lit area sent a shiver down my neck as I snuck around the warehouse section of the docks. There weren't many workers milling about at this time of night, and most of them seemed distracted. I could easily get around and check some units. There was a slight chill in the air as I searched for clues. The sea breeze made me glad I opted for a black hoodie with matching pants and a beanie. I tucked my hands into my hoodie's pocket and pressed my ear to a few locked units. In the corner of my eye, I noticed a surveillance camera slowly panning back and forth. The bright red light signaled it was on and watching. I shrunk back and tried my best to be out of its radius. It looked on the cheaper side, so I was hoping if I stayed close to the units or in shadowy spots that I couldn't be spotted. I checked a few more, each one seeming vacant. There was nothing but silence, as far as I could tell.

On my third section of units, I was starting to feel like I'd wasted my time coming out here. With each row having around twenty units, ten on the front side and another ten on the back, I had already searched about sixty units. Feeling tired and defeated, I didn't have the patience to check five more sections. It probably wouldn't even be possible before the sun came up, especially since it took me almost two hours to search what I had so far. I figured one more section of units wouldn't hurt. It was only going on one in the morning, so I had a bit of time before I had to get out of there. While trudging along, I noticed one unit that stood out against the rest. Most were securely locked, opened completely, or closed but left unlocked. This unit was left open a crack, making me think someone may have left in a hurry.

I reached for the chromed handle but stopped when I noticed a reddish color smeared on it. I peered closer and confirmed my suspicion. The substance was dried blood. Suddenly, I was acutely aware of what kind of danger I was putting myself in, though it was probably a little too late for that epiphany. There was still time to turn back and tell the MDPD about my findings, but curiosity was getting the best of me. Reaching for the underside of the door, I lifted the metal door as far as I could, even with my tiptoes assisting me. I took my phone out, turned the flashlight mode on, and shined it inside the dark unit. The sight that greeted me made me throw a hand over my mouth. I took a few steps inside, and my nose started burning as it encountered the stenches that clashed awfully. I could feel my stomach churn as the odor continued to engulf my nostrils, making me want to add my own bodily fluids to the ones that already seemed to be here.

If I had to guess, the person who had been held in this unit was here for more than a few days. One corner seemed to have been used as a bathroom. In another corner, they lost their stomach contents. There was some blood splattered around the room, but nothing to suggest a murder. As I scanned the unit, a message in the far-left corner caught my attention. It was written in blood and appeared to be more recent than the other bloodstains. The color was brighter. The message seemed carefully written out, so the hostage must have had a decent amount of time to complete it. The simple four-letter word read, H-E-L-P. What poor soul wrote this? I hoped they were okay, but if they weren't here now, then they were more than likely long gone.

A hand gripped my shoulder, making me stiffen as a jolt of terror coursed through me. I did *not* want to end up as the next victim. I had to think fast. With adrenaline shooting through my veins, I twisted my body around to face the person behind me. I took a swing at them. Thankfully, my wild punch connected, making the person let go of me. I shined my light on the subject, finding a familiar face hunched over and gripping at his stubbled jaw. "Marco?"

He looked up at me as he massaged the spot where I slugged him at. With narrowed eyes, he groaned, "Why'd you hit me?"

"You grabbed my shoulder. How was I supposed to know it was you?"

"I guess you have a point. Where'd you even learn how to hit like that?"

"Bryan is my brother. You can assume that we had a few roughhousing matches as young kids. Plus, when I was trying to score this job, they advised me to sign up for some self-defense lessons in case I needed to protect myself."

"Well, they paid off."

"What are you doing here anyway?"

He stood back to his full height, wincing as he moved his jaw around a bit. "I could ask you the same thing."

"Fair point. But I asked you first."

"I assumed you'd come out here to look for that Ivan guy."

"How could you possibly know that? *I* didn't even know what I was going to do until a few hours ago."

"Call it a hunch, which is basically what my job entails ninety-five percent of the time."

"Is Bryan with you?"

"No, I thought I'd follow this hunch on my own."

I turned, shining a light on the message written on the wall. "Looks like someone was here."

"There's no doubt about that," Marco said as he scrunched his nose. "And I hate to say it, but this isn't even the worst I've smelled."

"That's hard to imagine."

"Let's just say, a decomposing body left to rot inside a vent over the hot summer in Miami for two weeks, is not a great smell."

I wrinkled my nose. "Ugh. . . That sounds disgusting."

"Yeah, tell me about it." He crouched down next to the message on the wall, taking a closer look. "Seems fresh, maybe a day old. Could even be from this morning."

"That's what I was thinking. The blood's coloring looks fresher than some of the other bloodstains in here."

"Good eye, Dane."

"Are you going to call it in?"

Marco stood as he nodded. "Yeah, this is just the evidence

we need to obtain a warrant, so we can search this place from top to bottom."

A noise from outside caught our attention. By the time we turned to see who was outside, the roll-up door was being yanked down. We both sprinted toward the now-closed door, banging on the metal structure in hopes of getting out of the cramped and smelly space. Marco lunged for the bottom of the door, trying to lift it, but it was no use. We were trapped. The storage unit would now be pitch black if not for the small stream of light still being produced by my phone. The room was making me uneasy, my heart racing faster and faster as realization struck me. We were stuck in there. I reached for the concrete wall next to me, making contact with the cool surface as my breathing became ragged.

"Hey, are you okay?" I could faintly hear Marco ask from beside me.

"The room. . . It's small. It's hot," I mumbled as I tried to clutch at the flat surface beneath my hand.

"You're telling me you're claustrophobic?"

"Not necessarily. There are moments when it flares up, and being in a dark, windowless concrete box that smells like human waste is definitely something that would trigger it."

Marco turned me to face him, both hands on my shoulders. I could barely make out his facial features in the faint light, but he seemed concerned. "Look. I know this is terrifying, but I need you to try and stay calm for me. I learned this a long time ago from my therapist when I was young. During a panic or anxiety-induced attack, breathing techniques can help."

I shook my head, my chest tight as I struggled to inhale. "I can't. . . I can't even breathe."

"Sure you can. Trust me." He looked into my eyes and

whispered, "Close your eyes, and focus on my instructions."

I did as he said and waited for his next words. It didn't take long before he continued, "Breathe in through your nose as slowly and calmly as you can. Do your best not to take too much air in and try to relax."

I heard him counting under his breath, reaching the number five before instructing, "Breathe out through your nose in a similar fashion to how you breathed in, and count to five."

I followed his instructions once again, and we repeated the technique about three times before I started to feel slightly better. My palms were still clammy, my stomach knotted up, but I didn't feel like I was going to pass out. Suddenly nervous about being in such close proximity to Marco after a somewhat intense and vulnerable moment, I took a small step back and said, "Thank you for that. I feel a little better now."

"You're welcome. Panic attacks are no joke," he said as he rubbed a hand behind his neck.

"How are we going to get out of here?"

"I'll call Bryan and let him know where we are." Marco took out his phone, releasing an audible groan of frustration as he examined the screen. "I guess we aren't going to be calling anybody."

"What? Why?" I asked, trying to peek at his phone.

"No signal."

I checked my phone's screen, noticing a giant red X beside my bars with small wording that read, No Signal. "You've got to be kidding me."

"I guess we'll be stuck in here for a while."

"Is there anything else we can do?"

"I'm afraid not. The best thing we can do is wait."

"What if the person who locked us in here comes back?"

"Then they'll have to deal with me and my firearm."

"You have your gun?" I gestured to the locked door and asked, "Can't you just shoot us out of here?"

"This isn't the movies," he explained. "First of all, I have no idea where the lock is located. Shooting blindly at the door would do more harm than good. Second, since we're in such close range with the steel door in this tight unit, shooting at the target could cause the bullet to ricochet and hit one of us. I'd much rather go toe to toe with a potential gang member than one of my own bullets."

"I didn't think about that." With a defeated sigh, I whispered, "I just want to get out of here."

"Don't worry, all right? I'll protect you, no matter what happens."

I scrunched my eyebrows. "Why?"

He smirked. "I know Bryan would kill me if I didn't."

Hours passed as Marco and I sat in the sweltering, confined space. The smell was still unbearable, but after spending so much time there, my gag reflex seemed to have died down. The two of us were sweating profusely as we sat on the coolish concrete floor. About an hour in, we started to slowly undress ourselves. Marco had taken off his suit jacket and was now in a white dress shirt that was fully unbuttoned, revealing a white tank underneath. I took off my hoodie and was left with a thin-strapped black tank top along with my matching bra. Both of our phones died soon after that, and we were now enshrouded in complete darkness. My eyes were trying to adjust from the lack of light, but there wasn't much to see anyway. The silence was starting to get the best of me, so I struck up a conversation with Marco.

"Since we'll probably be stuck in here for a few more hours, I think we should get to know each other."

"I guess it wouldn't hurt," his voice rumbled from the left side of me. "Ask away, Ms. Dane."

"Let's start with something simple. What made you want to become a detective?"

"That's kind of complicated."

"Really? Here I thought it'd be easy."

"Let's just say that it touches on a personal aspect of my life that I'd rather not get into. I'll leave the answer brief and say that I witnessed a crime take place a long time ago. I felt the detectives involved did a crappy job, and I wanted to do it better. I wanted to give a voice to those who could no longer speak and seek justice for them."

"That's kind of sweet, Marco. And I'm sorry for whatever happened."

Dropping the subject, he said, "I guess it's my turn, huh?"

"Yes, ask me anything."

"I guess I'll piggyback off of yours. Why a forensic artist?"

"Mine is definitely simpler than yours. I lost my main freelancing gig and didn't have the time or money to try to pick up another one that would pay the bills. So, Bryan suggested becoming a forensic artist, at least until I could find something more stable."

"There wasn't anything else available?"

"Not that I could find. Most places were looking for years of experience, and others didn't seem to fit my personality."

"What's your dream job?"

"To work for myself I presume. I would love to sell my

artwork on my own website, or at a gallery, maybe even my own gallery if I'm lucky."

"What's stopping you?"

I laughed and said, "Money for starters. My marketing skills are a bit lackluster too, so selling myself, along with my artwork, is easier said than done."

"Can't your parents help?" Marco asked.

"Well, they never saw my art as a potential profession. They'd be terrified of investing in my business since it could potentially flop."

"That's a shame. Sometimes it's nice to take a chance on someone. You'll never know where it might lead."

"Would your parents help you?"

"If they had the money, I don't doubt that they would have done everything in their power to help me and my siblings."

"You have siblings?"

"My older brother, Fernando, and younger sister, Catalina. I had an older sister, Marta, but. . . she passed. My father also died after a sudden brain aneurysm about six years ago."

"I'm so sorry. Are you close to your family?"

I heard him shift slightly. "Not as much as when we were younger. My brother rarely comes around anymore, but I try to see my sister and mom when I can."

"I'm pretty close to Bryan and my dad. My mom and I have our moments, but we tend to butt heads pretty often."

"Your brother does seem to love you a lot. He would talk about you sometimes, especially when we first started."

"He did?"

"Yes, he always sounded proud of his little sister."

I smiled to myself. "How long have you known Bryan?"

"Since he joined the force. We were both beat cops during

our rookie years, me being about a year ahead of him. We worked our way up and eventually became detectives as well as partners." Marco's short chuckle broke through the darkness. "Do you know what happened when we first met?"

"What?"

"I thought your brother was Hispanic. Judging from his tanned complexion and facial features— and it is Miami after all— I just assumed he could speak Spanish like me. I went up to him and started to speak my native tongue, since I'm Puerto Rican. I'll never forget the look of confusion on Bryan's face as he tried to comprehend what I was saying."

"Oh my goodness. That is hysterical," I said, fighting through my own fit of laughter. "I'd be lying if I didn't say that it's happened to me several times throughout school and even into adulthood."

"I guess it's easy to be mistaken these days, no matter who you are or what you may look like."

"I guess that's a good thing," I said, grinning.

"I'd like to think so."

Remembering where we were, I decided to cut our fun short, getting back to our main predicament. "Do you think they'll find us?"

Marco hummed and replied, "Yes I do. I'm sure once Bryan or the MDPD can't get a hold of us, they'll start searching. This would definitely be one of the first places they'd look."

Silence fell between us again as my mind drifted to the hundreds of different scenarios that could play out. I believed Marco knew what he was talking about and that he could handle any situation that may arise, but I was still terrified by the creeping sensation that we wouldn't be found in time.

Chapter 16

I started to stir, waking up from the impromptu slumber that had overtaken me. It had been well over twenty-four hours since I had gotten some real sleep, and I was running on fumes. By now, most of my adrenaline had worn off, the exhaustion setting in. I lifted my head, noticing that it had landed on Marco's shoulder. Not knowing whether he was awake and feeling embarrassed, I mumbled a small, "Sorry."

To my horror, Marco answered, "Don't worry about it. I fell asleep for a bit too. It's not like we have anything else to do while we're in here."

"How long do you think we've been trapped here?"

"A rough estimate, possibly six hours or so. I'm sure the sun's already up by now."

"That was my thought too."

"I'm sure Bryan is already looking into it. They'll find us in no time."

My stomach clenched. "I sure hope you're right."

"I've been in tougher jams than this. They'll find us."

I paused before asking, "Can you tell me about them, or is it classified?"

"I'm not CIA, so I'm sure I can tell you about one of my more harrowing cases."

"What happened?"

"A couple of years ago, we were working on a case that took place at Miami Haven Zoo."

"I loved that zoo as a kid. My favorite exhibit was the lemurs."

"I used to enjoy it too, until that day, when Bryan and I decided to split up to cover more ground while searching for some evidence. I happened to find my way into the Florida panther exhibit."

"How did you even manage that?"

"I have no idea. I think I saw the directions of the arrows wrong because I was looking for the staff room but wandered into the panther's den instead."

"Did they try to get you?"

"They certainly did. I wound up climbing on top of a large rock to reach an overhang they'd installed to provide shade to the panthers. I tried to stay as far back from the ledge as possible because those suckers were spry."

"Most cats are," I said with a laugh.

He groaned. "Yeah, but when they're fifteen times the size of a house cat, it's a lot more terrifying."

"I'm sure it is. How did you get out?"

"It felt like hours, but it was probably a good twenty minutes of watching those giant cats try to get their paws on me before Bryan finally showed up. He called the zookeepers, and they were able to coax the two felines into their dens so I could get out."

"That sounds like it was a close call."

"That was honestly the most scared I've been in a long time. Getting shot at, stabbed by a drug addict, and knocked unconscious with a wrench was nothing compared to those panthers."

"Did you wind up finding any evidence for the case you were working on?"

"Funny thing is, my wrong turn led us to stumble on a watch that the suspect had tried to ditch. I guess he hoped the panthers would mistake it for something edible."

"Wow. . . He probably would have had better luck giving it to a crocodile."

Marco let out a hearty chuckle, presumably catching my reference to *Peter Pan*. His laugh was cut short when a noise rose from outside the unit. Someone seemed to be fiddling with the lock outside. Marco jumped up from his spot, and I could hear him grabbing for his gun. I felt his breath on my face as he leaned close to me and whispered, "Get behind me."

I was quick to heed his command and huddled behind his larger frame. I tried peeking over his shoulder as we waited for the door to open, but it was hard to do when he stood at least six inches taller than me. A large *clank* came from outside, followed by a clattering sound. Soon, the metal door was being lifted, and the bright Miami sunlight flooded the once pitch-black unit. I could barely see, squinting as I tried to adjust to the new lighting situation.

Marco lifted his gun at the figure standing in front of us, and a familiar voice called out, "Woah, don't shoot. It's me."

Marco lowered his weapon as I stepped away to see Bryan standing at the entrance. He was holding a bright-red bolt cutter and wore a look of concern. I rushed over to my older brother, wrapping my arms around him. He hugged me back as I mumbled into his shirt, "I've never been so happy to see you."

"Same here, Cal," he said.

Marco stepped over to us. "When did you realize we were here?"

"After we left Callie yesterday, I was worried she might do something foolish." His eyes narrowed on me before continuing, "When I got up this morning, I tried to call her. It kept going straight to voicemail. I called my parents and Natalie, and they said they hadn't seen her since yesterday. Then, I tried to call you and got the same thing as when I called Cal. I had an inkling you'd be here, but not trapped in a storage unit."

I gestured toward the bolt cutters in his hand. "And you just happened to have bolt cutters."

Bryan shrugged as he looked the tool over. "Old Bolty here is always in the trunk of my car. You never know when you need to pop some locks."

I smirked. "At least it's more practical than a taco-themed party shirt."

"Leave my taco shirt out of this."

Marco chuckled. "How'd you know what unit we were in?"

"That took longer than I'd thought. I wound up hearing you two chatting and couldn't mistake your voices."

"Did you call it in?"

"Not yet. I wanted to make sure I had solid evidence before calling out a squad." Bryan walked into the dank unit, putting the back of his hand up to his nose as he gagged. "Did you two do all this within the six hours you were in here?"

I scoffed. "Yes, Bry. We did all of this."

"Okay, don't bite my head off. Do you know who did?"

"No. They were gone by the time I got here."

A small bang came from the unit directly across from us. The three of us turned our heads toward the unexpected sound. Marco cautiously crept in that direction, and the two of us followed. When we reached the unit, another short, minimal bang echoed on the metal door. I looked at the two men. "Do you think there's someone in there?"

Bryan lifted his bolt cutter and said, "Only one way to find out."

He went over to the padlock, clipping the metal piece with ease. Once he discarded the cut lock, Marco lifted the door to the other unit. A young girl with matted, honey-blonde hair shrank back from us. She was covered in grime and was shaking violently as she cried. "Please, don't hurt me. Please. . ."

Marco flashed his badge and said, "We're not going to hurt you. We're with the MDPD, and we're here to help you."

"You are?"

"Yes. What's your name?"

"Amber. . . Amber Oliva."

The name sounded familiar. Then it hit me, where I had heard it before. It was at our first briefing on the case. Captain Baker mentioned he had a niece who had gone missing and was known to run with the gang.

Bryan must have must have recognized the name too because he asked, "Do you know Captain Drew Baker?"

She nodded. "That's my uncle."

I gasped and said, "So, she is the missing niece he was talking about."

"They're looking for me?"

I gave her a soft smile. "Of course. They're worried about you."

"I feel so dumb. I trusted my boyfriend, Felix. He said he could help me make quick money. It started with some drug sales. Next thing you know, I'm getting tossed into a trunk and taken here. I wasn't the only one either."

Marco asked, "There were more?"

"Yes, at least five."

"What happened to them?"

"No clue. They started getting pulled out one by one throughout the last week or so."

Bryan sighed. "I'm going to call this in. Marco, stay with Amber. Callie, I need to talk to you for a second."

Marco nodded as he slowly made his way over to Amber. I followed Bryan away from the unit so we could talk out of earshot. As Bryan took out his phone, he said to me, "I want you to go home."

"Don't you want a statement or something? And we still haven't found Ivan," I said.

"You're still undercover. Most employees are probably here by now. If you get caught, your cover will be blown."

"How do we know it's not already?"

"We don't. I just feel it would be better for you to go home. We'll have you come to the precinct after we get this place shut down and secured for the day."

"Fine. Will you let me know if you find anything on Ivan?"

"I will."

"I'll see you later, Bry."

"Okay," he murmured, his phone pressed to his ear. I started walking away when I heard Bryan call out, "And be careful!"

"I'll try," I called back.

I weaved in and out of pallets and freights as I tried to sneak out of the warehouse facility. I had no idea what time it was, but my shift had to have started by now. The majority of the loading dock was swarming with workers, some driving forklifts and others carrying cardboard boxes to their rightful destinations. I thought I'd be spotted once I reached the side entrance, but everyone seemed completely oblivious as they worked. With shocking effortlessness, I made it to my scooter in the parking garage across the way. Not wasting any time to test my luck further, I jumped onto my electric vehicle and rode to my parents' house.

Before I even managed to get through the front door, a flurry of arms wrapped around me. My mother was the first to pull away as my dad continued to squeeze the life out of me.

"Let the poor girl breathe, Harold," my mother said, sounding exasperated.

He pulled away with reluctance and mumbled, "I'm just glad my snuggle bug is okay."

"Yes, we all are." My mother turned to me and asked, "What were you thinking, going off on your own like that?"

I groaned. "All I wanted to do was search for a missing friend. Bryan and Marco wouldn't look into it, so I did. I didn't think I'd wind up getting trapped in a storage unit, but at least Marco was there to keep me company."

"Detective Suárez, your brother's partner? What was he doing with you?"

"He figured I wouldn't let things go and happened to run into me while I was there."

My dad let out a breath and said, "I'm glad someone was with you. Who knows how it could have ended?"

"It all worked out." Starting toward the stairway, I glanced back and said, "If you don't mind, I'm going to take a shower and a short nap before I have to head to the precinct later today."

"All right, baby girl. Would you like me to make you anything to eat?"

"No, thank you. I'm not that hungry."

I took my time climbing each step as my long day started to settle in, leaving me feeling fatigued and achy. I could vaguely hear my parents discussing something downstairs as I reached the landing. They were probably talking about the dangerous predicament I had put myself in, but I ignored their banter as I dragged my feet to my room. When I opened my door, I was once again forced into a gripping hug. Natalie pulled away with a look of relief.

"I'm so happy you're okay."

"What are you doing in my room?" I asked.

"I tried to wait it out with your family for a bit downstairs, but I thought your parents might have wanted to wait alone. So, I came up here."

"Thanks for staying with them."

"No problem. That's what friends do."

"I thought you might've had to work today."

"Not until five tonight." Natalie grabbed my arm pulling me to sit with her on my bed. "Now, tell me everything. What happened?"

"I was trying to find Ivan, the guy I work with, since he's missing."

"Any luck?"

"None. I did wind up finding a storage unit where someone had been held prisoner."

Her eyes flew wide. "That's wild."

"Marco figured that I'd be there, and we wound up getting trapped together when someone closed the unit from outside."

"You got trapped with your brother's hunky partner?" Natalie gasped with excitement. "Did anything happen?"

I shook my head with a faint chuckle. "No, nothing happened. We were surrounded by human waste and blood."

"Okay, ew. . . I guess that'd be a mood killer, but hey, if there was a possibility of dying, what would it hurt?"

I gave her a hard stare. "I barely know the guy."

"That never stopped me."

"Nat, focus."

"All right." She paused, pursing her lips. "So, what *did* you two do while you were stuck together?"

"We talked. He helped me settle down from a panic attack since I was feeling slightly claustrophobic."

"I didn't know you were claustrophobic."

"I'm not. . . not really. I had an episode once when I was riding my bus back home from my high school. We had to jam an extra person into a few of the seats because the bus was full. That meant three people on a seat meant for two, with the South Florida heat raging outside. The bus was so hot and stuffy, and I was feeling trapped. Since then, some small or crowded spaces get to me, especially when it's hot. But it's not as bad as some people have it, people who have an actual diagnosis."

"Wow, I didn't know that. And Marco helped you through it?"

"Yep. He helped me stay calm."

Natalie smirked and said, "I think you like him."

"What? I don't like him. He's not as terrible as I thought when I first met him, but I don't think of him as any more than a colleague. He's also my brother's partner. It'd be weird."

She tilted her head, still smiling. "Whatever you say."

"I really came up here to take a shower and get some shuteye after my long day."

"Copy that. I should also take a short nap before my shift starts." Natalie hopped up and strolled toward my bedroom door. "By the way, I'm glad you're okay."

"Thanks. I'm glad Bryan was able to find us in time."

When Natalie left, I was finally alone to manage my thoughts. I plugged my phone in as I replayed last night on a loop in my mind. I was grateful that Marco had been with me during that ordeal. Who knows if I'd have been able to handle it alone? I'm sure they still would have found me eventually, but what if it would have ended up differently? Especially if the person who locked us in had seen one trespasser instead of two. My phone buzzed multiple times as it turned back on, all my messages and phone calls coming through now that it had juice and a signal. I skimmed through them, most having come from Bryan, my parents, and Natalie. I had one voicemail from my loading-docks job, which only came in about an hour ago.

Pressing play, I listened to the automated message before heading to my shower. "Employees of Conwell's Oceanic Shipping Company, we are closing down today due to a heavy police presence. We were instructed to keep everyone away from the area while they conduct their investigation. We are unaware of how long this will take, so until there is an all-clear, please do not report to work. We will send another message when it's safe to return. If you have further questions, please call your supervisor or our main office at 188- Conwell's-Co. Goodbye."

I felt a flood of relief that the place was shut down, at least for today. I just hoped it was enough to spare me of suspicion. After deleting the voicemail, I took a comforting shower before getting some much-needed rest.

Chapter 17

In the middle of my nap, my phone began buzzing up a storm on my childhood nightstand. I turned over in my bed, grabbing for the pestering device that had roused me from my blissful sleep. After getting hold of it, I didn't even check the caller ID before I swiped at the green answer button. I ran a hand down my face and asked with a yawn, "What?"

"Were you sleeping?" Bryan asked me on the other end.

"Yes. It's been a very long day. Actually, make it a long month."

"Well, don't worry. This should be over soon. We've just apprehended a seventh Lucifer's Losers member. Most of them aren't speaking, which isn't a shocker, but we should be able to get enough evidence to convict them all."

"Do you know who the leader is yet?"

"That's our biggest roadblock as of now. No one's going to

rat out their leader, no matter how good of a deal we offer them. They'd much rather rot in prison than be targeted for the rest of their lives."

"Am I still in danger?"

"That's why I called you. We searched every unit at the warehouse, including some shipping containers. We found Ivan in one of them."

I jolted to a sitting position, now fully awake as my nerves prickled with worry. "Is he okay? Please tell me he's alive."

Bryan sighed. "He is for now. We had to have the paramedics rush him to the ER. The guy looked like he went several rounds with an angry bull, so it wasn't pretty. It seems like he lost a couple of digits too."

"That's awful. He'll pull through, right?"

"It's hard to say. Depending on the main extent of his injuries, he could live, or. . ."

My heart sank. "Do you think I can go see him?"

"You can try. Hospitals are pretty strict about that sort of thing when you aren't immediate family or police."

"I am technically with the police."

"You can swing by and give it a shot. He's at Miami General, and if they ask you for proof, tell them to call Captain Baker. He'll probably vouch for you. I'd bring your sketchbook too, so you seem legit."

"Will do. Thanks for the update, Bryan."

"No problem." Before I could hang up, my brother stopped me with another quick message. "Oh, and about being in danger. I'd still keep an eye out. We don't know what information Ivan may have given away, so stay alert and stay safe, Cal."

I nodded, even though he couldn't see me. "I will. Don't

worry."

With a short goodbye, we hung up our call. I was happy to hear that Ivan had been found alive, but I wished Bryan, Marco, and the MDPD would have taken my claims seriously in the first place. It might have spared Ivan from the obvious torture he had endured in the last forty-eight to seventy-two hours. Knowing that nothing would change the past, I hopped out of bed and got ready to visit him in the hospital.

I arrived at Miami General Hospital with my sketchbook in hand. I was determined to see Ivan today, so I hoped the plan Bryan had suggested would work out. I reached the front desk of the busy hospital, their phones ringing nonstop while several people stood in line either to check in or to get a visitor's pass. Even though the place was a bit chaotic, the workers remained calm, keeping everything running smoothly. The line dwindled faster than I had anticipated, and it was eventually my turn.

A young woman, presumably around my age, took me at her station and asked, "How may I help you, ma'am?"

"I'm here to visit someone who was brought in earlier today," I said, my throat suddenly dry.

"Can I have the name of the patient you're visiting?"

"Ivan."

"Last name?"

My mind blanked. I didn't know his last name. Marco and Bryan had mentioned it once when they were warning me about his record, but it hadn't crossed my mind that I'd need to remember it. Wracking my brain, I stumbled over a few possibilities, recalling that it started with the letter C. "Canto?"

"No, we have no one by that name," she said, shaking her head.

"Carno, maybe?"

"Mm, no."

"Carrano… Ivan Carrano," I said, a light bulb seeming to go off at the thought.

"Ah, yes. He came in a few hours ago with some serious injuries."

"Can I see him?"

"I'm assuming you're not family, nor a significant other, so I'm going to have to say that you can't see him at this time."

"I'm with the MDPD. You can call my supervisor, and here's my ID badge." I handed the woman a business card with Captain Baker's number along with my ID that I received when I joined the MDPD.

"I don't think questions are going to be possible right now."

"I'll be quick. I'm just here to sketch a few details. I'm more of a forensic artist than a detective."

She chewed on her lip as if thinking it over. "Give me one second."

The woman slipped into the back with the items I'd given her, and I patiently waited as I watched other people being attended to. Before long, she returned and handed my stuff back to me. I watched her type something up before a gray visitor's badge was printed out. She detached it from the printer and handed it over. "You have thirty minutes to get what you need. He's in the ICU on the third floor, room 311."

"That's enough for me. Thank you," I said as I took the visitors badge and placed the sticker on my shirt.

After taking the elevator to the third floor, I found Ivan's room with ease. It was hard to see him hooked up to all the machines as he lay motionless in his bed. Surprisingly, he only had a nasal oxygen tube rather than a ventilator tube down the throat. I guess that meant he wasn't too hurt and could breathe relatively well. I cautiously sat down in the hard vinyl chair, which was a horrible salmon color. The pen and pencil in my pocket were digging into my thigh as I sat, so I pulled them out. I placed atop my sketchpad as I watched Ivan rest.

He was littered with bruises from his face to his hands. I was sure the parts I couldn't see were just as bad. The contusions were all different shades. Some were black and blue while others were a deep purple. A few were a dark, angry red. His left eye was swollen shut, and his left hand had a bandage wrapped around it. I noticed his pinky and ring finger were missing, remembering what my brother said about him losing a few digits. A pit of guilt settled in my stomach even though it wasn't truly my fault. I just wished I could have gotten to him sooner.

My heart leapt when Ivan's head lolled over to me. His good eye studied me with curiosity until I could see the realization hit him. With a weak smirk, he asked, "What are you doing here?"

"When my detective brother said they had found you, I just had to come see you," I answered as I wrung my hands.

"You didn't need to do that."

"I know, but I wanted to." I looked over his battered body and asked, "How are you feeling, by the way?"

"Not bad, even with the loss of two fingers. I'm just happy they were my least used fingers and on my non-dominant hand."

"I'm glad you're in good spirits, even after what happened."

"It could have been worse. . . They could have easily killed me."

I gulped, my throat going dry again. "I just wish we could have found you sooner. I tried to tell the detectives that you were in danger, but they were still wary of you because of your record."

"Oh, geez. I knew that would haunt me for the rest of my life. Those are definitely moments I regret."

"Can you tell me about them?"

He drew a deep breath. "I got an aggravated assault charge after getting into a fight with my stepdad a few years ago. I never liked the way he treated my mom, so when we were tussling in their yard, I grabbed one of my mom's gnomes and slammed it into his head twice, knocking him unconscious. My grand-theft charge was when I was nineteen, dumb and with even dumber friends. I was the only one who knew how to hotwire a car and was behind the wheel when we got pulled over."

"Were you ever convicted in either case?"

"My grand theft, yes. I did get my charges dropped on the aggravated assault because my mother blackmailed my stepdad. She threatened to leave him and tell the police about his side hustle that he had stashed away in their closet."

"Did you ever think about getting those records expunged?"

"I have. . . I tried looking into it, but the whole process seemed a bit convoluted, to say the least. I might be able to get them off my record, but since I was convicted on the one, I might not have any luck."

I leaned in closer. "Maybe I can get my brother to pull some strings."

"That would be great. It'd help me a lot."

I opened my sketchbook and added, "Even though I came here to see you personally, I should still get some information from you for my job."

He gave me a slow nod. "I understand. What do you want to know?"

"Any details on who was torturing you and what they looked like. I'm sure we'll have to go over this again another day so we have more time to get a more concise sketch. But just give me a general idea."

"For a while, it was just two guys. One had thin brown hair, and the other was bald. The brown-haired dude had a slender and long face, eerily narrow brown eyes, and a goatee. His resting expression was a scowl. The other dude was built like an ox. He had a thick, square-cut jawline and a couple of moles around his face. One was by his nose and the other near his temple."

"Then someone else came?"

"Yup. . . Two others. One was Red."

A shudder coursed through me. "Red stopped by?"

"Yes, she came on the second day. At least I think it was. Time was kind of funny then."

"Did she ask you anything?"

"The same things the other two did— if I knew what they did and who the mole was. I tried my best to hold out, but it was a struggle, especially when the last guy came."

"Is he the one who took your fingers?"

"He was. He was tall, muscular, but older than the lot of them. He wore dark gloves and had an eyepatch. His light-gray hair was slicked back as well. Honestly, he seemed like a straight-up villain out of a thriller."

"He sounds terrifying."

"Even Red seemed intimidated by him. I think it was her father, but I could barely make out what they were saying at the time."

I cocked my head to the side. "Father? But Mr. Conwell has been dead for years. At least, that's what I've heard. And if he was Mr. Conwell, that also means Red is Kris Conwell, the owner of the company."

"Huh. . . I could be wrong, but considering the way he berated her and told her she couldn't handle his company, that would make sense."

"If he is alive, that means he faked his death."

"He probably wanted to run things from the sidelines. Keeping himself on the down-low would let him do more dirty deeds without getting caught."

"Exactly. I'm going to have to tell the MDPD this news." It was a new twist in the case, one the department had thought very unlikely. "Did you tell them about me?"

He sighed, glancing away from me. "I did. I'm sorry. I tried to hold out, but after losing my last finger and getting punched and beaten for over two hours, I was drained. I just wanted it to stop."

"There's no need to apologize. I doubt I could have lasted half as long as you did."

"I just hope I helped you enough to catch them before they get to you."

I nodded, feeling a surge of confidence. "I think the police force will be able to nab them with the information you just gave me."

"I'm glad I could be useful."

"Thank you, Ivan. They'll probably have you come down to the station or come up here like I did to get more information. But for now, it seems like enough."

"That's fine. Anything to get some lowlife scum off the streets."

I closed my sketchbook after writing down all the details Ivan had just told me. Not wanting to leave quite yet, I asked, "What are you going to do if the warehouse shuts down?"

"I wasn't thinking of staying there much longer anyhow. For the last week, I've been searching job sites to see if I can make my way up to becoming a chef. Looked into some culinary schools, too, so I can take classes while I'm working."

"I hope it works out for you. I know chasing a dream is hard."

He shot me a half-smile. "I think we still have time to achieve them."

"I guess you're right. It's never too late."

I started to leave, and Ivan stopped me before I could move away from his bedside. "I was wondering if you'd want to have dinner with me next weekend. The doctors said if I keep improving, I can potentially get out on Wednesday. I would still love to cook for you."

I smiled at him, dipping my head. "You know, why not? I think it'd be nice."

"Can we call it a date, or is it still two co-workers hanging out?"

"Well, since we're technically no longer co-workers, I think we can call it a date."

His eyes brightened as a grin stretched across his bruised face. "A date it is, then."

I flipped open my sketchpad and scribbled my number on the corner of one blank sheet. I tore it out before placing it on the rolling table next to Ivan's bed. "Call me when you can."

"I will."

I gave him a short wave goodbye before stepping out of his room. I wasn't necessarily looking for anyone to date right now, but sometimes, if it feels right, you have to just go for it. And it felt right with Ivan. On the way to my scooter, I tried to figure out where my next stop would be. My best bet would be the precinct, but I was still a bit groggy from the whole warehouse ordeal. Before I could make a choice, a text message came through.

I checked my phone, seeing it was from my mother. *"Can you come home? I have something I need to discuss with you."*

I hummed to myself, wondering what my mother could have possibly needed to talk about. She probably wanted to know more about my risky endeavor yesterday. She'd more than likely try to get me to quit, even if it was a better job than my temporary art gigs. I texted her back, *"I'll be home soon."*

"Okay, honey."

I looked at the last text, puzzled. My mother never called me honey. It was always Callie, dear, or sweetie. Mounting my bike with hesitation, I continued to ponder the random texts. Pushing my better judgment aside, I decided to drive home to see what was going on.

Chapter 18

When I got to my parents' place, something felt off. Ever since that uncharacteristic text from my mother, that little feeling in the pit of my stomach kept nagging at me. Surveying the neighborhood, I noticed an unfamiliar car parked near our neighbor's driveway across the street. It could have been anyone, but I knew it wasn't a coincidence that a random car would be parked across the street after what happened at the docks. I peered more closely, trying to catch a glimpse of the vehicle's interior, but the windows were too tinted to make anything out. My phone vibrated in my pocket, startling me from my thoughts. With a shaky hand, I reached for my phone to check who was calling. To my relief, it was just Bryan. I answered it without hesitation. "What's up, Bryan?"

"Where are you?" he rushed out.

"I just got back to our parents' house. Why?"

"We got someone to take a deal, and they confessed a good chunk of information. We went to the headquarters of Conwell's shipping company to bring Red— Kris Conwell— down for questioning, and she's not here. No one has seen her today."

"You know Red is Kris?"

"Yep. After more digging and some snippets from our lovely snitch, we pieced it together. We also got a hit back on the fingerprints we lifted from the card you received, and they were a match. You're lucky you made it out of that meeting with her."

"I don't think I was that lucky." I glanced over at the out-of-place vehicle and thought about the strange text I'd received after leaving the hospital. "I think I know where she is."

"How? Where?"

"In our house. I got a mysterious text from Mom a little while ago. I have a feeling Red is in there with Natalie and our parents as hostages."

"Are you sure?"

I clenched my jaw. "I'm positive."

"Stay where you are. We'll be there in twenty minutes."

"There's one more thing."

"What?"

I drew a shaky breath. "Vince Conwell is alive."

"He can't be. He died."

"Ivan swore that one of the men who tortured him was Red's father. The only explanation is that Vince is alive."

"If that's the case, then things just got a whole lot more difficult."

I looked back at my parents' home, determination sparking inside me. "I'm going in, Bry."

"Don't even think about it. You're going to get yourself killed."

"I can distract them until you get here. I'm sure they heard me arrive anyway."

"I guess I can't stop you." He breathed out a somber groan. "Just be careful, okay?"

"I will."

"See you soon."

We hung up, and I braced myself for what awaited me inside. I hoped this scheme wasn't about to get me and my family killed. Red and her gang were only after me anyway. I was the one who tried to infiltrate their whole operation. They should only be targeting me, but I'm sure that's not how gangs function. With every step I took up to the front door, my nerves continued to rise, my body trembling. Anything could be behind this door. My parents and Natalie could already be dead for all I knew. I steadied my hand on the bronze handle, trying to keep myself calm before I pushed it open. The door was barely opened before I was thrown to the ground with brute force.

My head throbbed as I lay on the cool marble flooring of my parents' foyer. A pair of strong, thick hands were forcing my arms behind my back, and I felt a rough piece of rope being wound around my wrists. The person knotted it tightly, the rope digging into my skin. I tried to focus on the area around me, but my vision was blurred as my head continued to pound. A pair of black-heeled boots stepped into my vision. I struggled to look up at the person in front of me. Though it was difficult, I managed to lift my gaze. It was Red. I wasn't surprised to see her standing over me, her face contorted with rage.

She snapped her fingers at the person who was still behind me, and said, "Get her up, Hugo."

A faint "Yes, ma'am," was all I heard before I was yanked off the ground. I barely caught my footing as I was forced upright. Red stepped closer, making me shrink back. A sinister smirk parted her ruby-red lips as she tilted her head to the side. Her steel-blue eyes narrowed on me, a chaotic chuckle erupting from her mouth. "Did you really think I wouldn't catch on, Callie Duncan? Or should I say, Dane?"

I shrugged, putting on a display of confidence. "I tried to be optimistic."

"Cute. . ." A hand whipped across my face, making my head jerk to the right side. My cheek was on fire, and the throbbing in my head only got worse. "You destroyed everything."

"It's not my fault you're running the sick and twisted company that your father built. Plus, I'd say I did a pretty good job if you only caught on now."

Her arm rose, her gloved hand tightening into a fist. I was ready for the punch, but before she could make contact, an older voice boomed, "Enough, Kris!"

With her punch inches from my face, she let out an annoyed sigh before lowering her fist. She turned toward the man who'd stopped her and said, "I have this under control."

The man stepped into my view. He looked exactly like the man Ivan mentioned when I'd questioned him. He had slick gray hair and an eyepatch. and lean muscles. A suave suit was stretched over his lean muscles, and like Red, he wore gloves. He towered over the woman in front of me with a look I knew all too well. A look of disappointment. A cutting expression that only a parent could be capable of. "Do you, my dear? Ever since I handed my company over to you, everything seemed to be going downhill. Now look where we are— on the verge of being shut down and arrested."

Red stared down at the floor before glancing back at the man I presumed to be her "dead" father. "If you hadn't had to fake your death because you got caught by the IRS and the CIA, then we wouldn't be here. You caused this too."

"You dare talk back to me, young lady? I have been nothing but good to you since you were born. The life of luxury and privilege. Without me, you'd be nothing."

"Maybe that's how I would rather have had it."

"If that's how you feel." He walked around her, now looming over my small frame. He may have been old, but I could tell he was still highly athletic and kept in shape. Which left me terrified about what could happen in the next fifteen minutes. He turned his head slightly toward his daughter. "Once this job is complete, I want you gone. You're no longer a part of this operation, or this family."

Red's expression morphed into a look of shock, her mouth agape. "You're disowning me?"

"That's what it seems it has come to. Now, stay with the others while I deal with the mole."

I could see Red was hesitant about letting the conversation end that way, but she reluctantly turned on her heels before sauntering toward the living room. I looked up at the one-eyed man standing in front of me. He had a fierce scowl plastered on his wrinkled face. "You're Vince Conwell?"

"Indeed I am." He folded his arms in front of his chest. "And you're a cop?"

"Actually, I'm a forensic artist."

"What the hell is that?"

"I draw criminals, or victims, to help the cops identify who they are looking for."

"You've got to be kidding me. You're not even a real cop, yet you take down my whole operation?"

"I mean, kind of. The MDPD was technically still helping with the case."

He sniggered. "You must be pretty dumb to get into something like this."

"No, just down on my luck."

"I know how that goes. Lost my eye to a nasty infection when I was twenty-eight and homeless. I vowed to never sink that low again. That's when I started my company."

"You smuggle drugs and traffic people. That's not something to be proud of."

Vince snorted, "Listen, I never said my hard work and money were going to be from legal endeavors. Those two things were, and still are, the biggest money makers I've seen in all my years of business. If I was still shipping out and bringing in pointless materialistic crap, I'd be in the negative. With my extra business on the side, I was creating an empire."

"Well, now it's going to be landing you behind bars."

"Not when they think I'm dead. I'll be a free man once this little job is finished."

"But there are witnesses who've seen you and can identify you. You can't hide forever."

He leaned closer to me and whispered, "Don't worry. I'll take care of that."

Vince's gloved hand wrapped around the back of my neck, and he thrust me forward. He led me to the living room where my mom, my dad, and Natalie were bound individually. The three of them were sitting equally spaced on the couch with their legs tied together and hands secured behind their backs.

When they saw me, all three of them started crying and yelling, but their cries were muffled by the duct tape over their mouths. I was glad they weren't dead, but who was to say that wasn't next on the agenda? As I'd predicted, Vince let go of my neck and took out a firearm with a silencer on it. My family soon piped down as they stared at the man with the weapon. He cocked his gun before meeting my eyes with a smug grin. "Now, who do you want to see go first?"

"What?" I asked in a shaky voice, though I knew exactly what he was asking.

"Who do you want me to put a bullet into first?" He walked down the line of the couch, aiming the gun at each person in turn. "Your dear mother, your father, or your friend?"

Dumbstruck, I stood completely still, trying to brainstorm a way out of this. My mind couldn't even comprehend what was going on as my body trembled with fear. I didn't know how much longer it'd be until Bryan and the rest of the MDPD showed up to save us, but stalling was getting more difficult by the second. I noticed Vince was getting irritated as he eyed me with a menacing glare. "You pick, or I pick. . . You have three seconds."

As he counted down, my mouth blurted out, "My brother!"

"I don't see no brother here. Now pick someone."

My brother was sneaking around a corner with his weapon drawn. A few officers were with him as they got into position. I knew we were about to be saved, so I decided to work on Vince's nerves. "I see my brother."

"Yeah? Where?"

"Right here," Bryan said as he trained his weapon on Vince. "You're all under arrest for murder, kidnapping, human trafficking, and drug smuggling."

"How did you even get in? I had my men guarding every entrance to this place."

"It helps that I know every inch of this place. Plus, your lackeys weren't that hard to take care of."

Vince raised his hands in surrender. "I knew I should have never hired those incompetent fools."

Cops swarmed into the room, but before I could feel relief, an arm grabbed me, pulling me back until I hit a slender body. The cool metal of a gun was pressed to my temple, and I could feel the blood draining from my face as fear once again swept over me. Vince looked over at his daughter, who was currently holding me at gunpoint. With an incredulous look, he stumbled out, "What in God's name do you think you're doing?"

"Something you wouldn't have the balls to do. You think I'm a disgrace, the worst thing to happen to your company? Then I'll show you how capable I am," I heard her sneer behind me.

"Nonsense. You're going to get yourself killed."

"I'll die fighting. Unlike you, who tried to hide away for the rest of your pathetic life."

"At least I got to live," he bellowed.

"That doesn't matter to me anymore."

Bryan stepped forward, his gun drawn at Red. "Drop it, Kris. This is over."

"No it's not," she replied, dragging me away from all the officers in the room.

She carefully pulled me back to the foyer as she staggered to the front door. She made sure to keep us facing the police in case they decided to try anything, at which moment she'd use me as her human shield. She had a firm grip around my waist as she continued to guide me to where she wanted to go.

When we reached the front door, she quickly fumbled with the handle, swinging the door open. Before we could make it out, another gun was pointed at us. With a cheeky smirk on his face, Marco asked, "Going somewhere?"

"Move," Red grumbled. "Move or I'll blow her brains out."

"I don't think so. You even flinch, and one of us will do the same to you."

I could feel Red's hesitation as her hand flexed around me several times in the span of a few seconds. Suddenly, her arm dropped from my waist, letting me go. Marco didn't waste any time as he grabbed my wrist, pulling me behind him. With his gun still trained on Red, he said, "Drop your weapon. Get on your knees, and put your hands behind your head."

She did as she was told, slowly hunching over to place her gun on the tiled floor and crawling onto her knees. Once she was on the ground, with her hands on her head, Bryan rushed up to her, kicking the gun away. He skillfully pulled her arms behind her back and cuffed them together. I had never seen my brother in action before. Witnessing what he does almost every day was a sight to behold.

Bryan rambled out the Miranda rights to Red before passing her off to a uniformed officer who was backing him up. As the officer led her to a squad car, Bryan jogged over to me, wrapping his arms around me in obvious relief. "Are you okay, Cal?"

"I'm good. A little shaken up, but good," I said with a sigh.

"I think you should get checked out anyway. That's a pretty nasty bruise on your face."

I tentatively touched the left side of my face, wincing at the sharp pain my touch elicited. Hugo must have thrown me down onto the tiled floor harder than I thought, and I'm sure the slap from Red didn't help. I nodded and said, "Maybe I should, just to be safe."

He gazed down at me with a caring smile that I didn't hesitate to return. "I'll take you to the hospital once everything is clear."

"Thanks."

"Anything for you." He glanced inside the house and said, "I'm going to check on Mom, Dad, and Natalie. You want to come?"

"In a second."

He gave me a short nod before heading inside, maneuvering around some officers who were filing out of the house. I looked over at Marco, who was watching as the other criminals, including Vince, were escorted out of my parents' home in handcuffs. Each one was placed in a separate squad car as officers talked among themselves. I meandered over to Marco and said, "I want to thank you for saving my life today."

He shrugged with a little shake of his head. "It's my job."

"I know, but if you hadn't been there, who knows what would have happened."

"It was all a part of the plan. There's always a runner in these situations. You just have to know how to deal with them."

"Well, thank you anyway. My brother has a great partner by his side."

In the spur of the moment, I pulled Marco into a quick hug. I felt him go rigid underneath me, probably surprised by the sudden affection. When I let go, I shot him a friendly smile before I made my way back inside. Upon entering the living room, I was met by happy gasps and cries as I was pulled into frantic embraces.

"You're all okay, right?" I asked as I looked my loved ones over.

My dad nodded. "Yes, but don't worry about us. What about yourself?"

"I'm fine. Only suffered this bruise." I pointed to my cheek.

"I'm glad to hear that."

My smile dropped as I grew serious. "I want to apologize for putting you all through this."

My mother came up to me, tenderly rubbing my arms. "This isn't your fault. You were just doing your job. A job you would have never had to take if I had supported you in the first place."

"Honestly, I'm kind of glad it did work out like this. This may not be the particular predicament I thought I'd find myself in when becoming a forensic artist, but it helped fuel my passion for art again. And I think I'm going to dive back into art until I get that gallery I always dreamed of."

My mother's eyes were glassy. "And I support that decision."

She pulled me into her embrace, and after countless long, exhausting years, I finally felt my mother and I were on the same page. When she let go, my father patted me on the back and said, "I support you too."

"Thank you both. I won't let you down, not this time."

"You'd never let us down."

Bryan waved over Marco, who was standing casually in the entryway to our living room. He meandered over to us, and Bryan asked him, "Can you take my parents to the hospital? I'll take Callie and Natalie in my car, and we'll meet you there."

"Sure thing," Marco said.

They followed him out, and Natalie came over to me. She nudged my arm and said, "You sure know how to turn your unadventurous life into a rollercoaster, I'll tell you that."

I let out a short chuckle. "I'm sorry I dragged you into this mess."

"Don't be. This was the most excitement I've had in weeks. Plus, I got to miss work, and that's always a win in my book."

"Of course it is."

Bryan swung an arm over my shoulder. "Let's get going. I don't want to make Marco wait; he can get pretty impatient."

I smirked. "That's not surprising."

"No, it really isn't." Bryan tilted his head to motion toward the doorway. "Come on, you two. The faster we get there, the quicker we can get this day over with."

The three of us left the house, cramming into Bryan's car to head to the hospital. As we pulled away from the curb, I noticed the officers who were still on scene securing the area, probably waiting on the crime scene unit to arrive to collect evidence. Leaning back in the seat, I thought about the way the case had ended. It wasn't ideal, but I was glad that my family and best friend had survived the traumatic experience I'd put them through. They could have all been dead right now, and I could have died right alongside them. But thankfully, it all worked out. I was just hoping if I did continue to work for the MDPD, this wouldn't be a recurring situation. That said, I was pretty sure my undercover days were over.

Chapter 19

After finishing up the whirlwind of a case I'd been sucked into, I was feeling relieved. Not once did I think that partaking in a forensic artist job would lead me into helping the MDPD take down a trafficking gang and corrupt corporation. Even though it had been tough, I enjoyed myself. On top of that, I felt that I'd actually accomplished something in my life. The experience even gave me back the inspiration I'd been lacking to finish some of my unfinished work and start on some new art projects. But those would have to wait for now. Because I had a meeting with the captain in a few minutes.

The whole weekend, as Natalie and I tried to reorganize our apartment after the break-in, I'd thought about what this meeting might be about. I was certain that I wouldn't be fired since I did help solve the case. But would I be sent back down to work as a police clerk, or given a permanent position as a forensic artist? I hoped I'd be awarded a permanent position, but I knew it might not be possible.

When I reached the captain's office, he greeted me with a warm smile and gestured to the chairs in front of his desk. As soon as I sat down, Captain Baker began, "I wanted to start this off with another heartfelt 'thank you.' I don't think we would have been able to pull this off without you, Ms. Dane. Today, my sister and her husband are able to hug Amber because you didn't give up on this case. I know it was rough at the start, dealing with multiple ups and downs, but you kept going."

"I'm glad to hear that she's doing well. I wanted nothing more than to see the case all the way through, and I'm happy I was able to save some lives because of it."

"You saved more lives than you know." The captain leaned forward and said, "Which brings me to my next subject. How would you like to be a full-time forensic artist with the Miami-Dade Police Department?"

For a moment, I was speechless. "Are you serious?"

"I most certainly am. After a long deliberation with the chief of police, police commissioner, other members of the board, and the mayor, we have decided to create a spot on our force for a forensic artist."

I set my shoulders back, a swell of pride filling my chest. "I'd be honored to take that spot, sir."

"I'm glad to hear it. You'll start tomorrow, and you'll even get your own office. It's small, but it'll suffice for the work you'll be doing."

"I can't wait."

"Get as much rest as you can today, because you'll have a lot of work to do from here on out, Ms. Dane."

"I won't let you down, Captain."

"I know you won't." He stood and said, "Would you like to see your new office?"

"Sure," I said as I followed him to my new work quarters.

It wasn't too far from his own office, and I even had a view of Bryan and Marco's desk in the bullpen. It was quite small, having only enough room for my desk, computer equipment, a couple of chairs, and a plant. But the upside was that I had a window. I couldn't complain about my new space. A job was a job, and that's just what I needed right now.

"If you'd like, you can spruce it up a bit before you head home," the captain mentioned.

"I think I will. It'll give me less to do tomorrow," I said as I continued to eye my new office.

"I'll let you get to it, then." He started to leave before turning back to say, "And once again, welcome to the team, Ms. Dane."

When he was gone, I gave a short fist pump of joy, seeing that some of my work had paid off. I may not have been showcasing my work in a gallery or running a successful art website, but I was using my gift to save lives and serve justice. I was starting to think this was much better than anything else I could have dreamed up in the past. I wouldn't change a thing.

"Excited about your new office, Cal?" Bryan snickered behind me.

"Very much so," I said, swinging around to face him. "Did you know?"

"The captain filled me in a little while ago. I couldn't be happier for you, though I was hoping to get a window office myself if I moved up the ladder."

"I'll let you borrow it sometime. Just don't mess it up."

"I'll take good care of it." Bryan hitched a thumb towards the doorway and said, "Before I head back to filling out paperwork, I wanted to ask if I could treat you to a celebratory dinner tonight."

"Sounds good, as long as you're not cooking," I said with a chuckle.

"Don't worry, I'm not. I know this fantastic Mexican restaurant down A1-A, and it's to die for."

"All right. Just don't wear that hideous taco shirt."

"Fine, it's your dinner night. Bring Natalie too, and we'll make it a party."

"How about Marco?"

Bryan raised an eyebrow, a smirk forming on his face. "Marco, huh?"

I crossed my arms and said, "It's not like that. But he helped as much as you did in this case. He may want to unwind."

"You can ask him, but he rarely takes time for himself. I've literally had to drag him out to have some fun. One time, I even had to tell him there was a dead body at the club to get him there."

"You're awful," I scoffed.

"It worked, and no harm was done." Bryan started to leave. "Well, I have some work to get done. And if you see Marco around, go ahead and ask him. Maybe he'll say yes."

I waved him off and said, "I will."

Taking a moment to gather my thoughts, I headed downstairs to get some of my things that were still in the records office. When I walked inside, Mabel's face lit up. "I didn't think you'd come back, sweet pea."

"I had no idea what was going to happen over the last two weeks," I said with a faint chuckle.

"Are you working down here again, or did you get that promotion?"

"They gave me a permanent forensic artist position."

"Well, good for you. I have some news too," she said with a secretive smile.

"What's that?"

"This'll be my last week as a record's clerk. I am fully retiring. Now, I get to spend the rest of my years hanging out with my children and watching my grandbabies grow up."

"I'm happy for you, Mabel. I know how much you wanted to spend more time with your family."

"Yep. It looks like we're both moving a step closer to our happiness."

"It sure does." I looked around and asked, "You don't happen to have an empty box I could use to lug my stuff upstairs, do you?"

"It so happens that I do." She got up from her desk and grabbed a box from the corner of the room. "I just emptied this today and was going to toss it."

I took the cardboard box from her and said, "Thank you. This will be perfect."

I started to throw in some of the knick-knacks on my desk that I had accumulated over my short time working there. I had a couple of family photos, a water thermos that probably needed a thorough cleaning, and a few favorite pens. Once I had all my stuff, I gave a heartfelt goodbye to my short-time, but impactful, friend I'd made in the records room. Mabel even surprised me with a short little hug and her number in case I needed a word of elderly advice that didn't come from my parents. I made my way back up to the homicide unit and found Marco sitting at his desk staring at a piece of paper. I detoured over to him, so I could ask if he wanted to join our dinner party tonight. When I walked up to his desk, he folded the paper, tossing a small polaroid inside of it. He hurriedly shoved it into his desk drawer before aiming his attention toward me.

"Are you okay?" I asked.

Marco nodded as he fixed his slim black tie. "Just a personal letter from an old friend. I wasn't expecting to hear from them."

"Well, I wanted to ask if you would like to tag along with me, Bryan, and my friend Natalie tonight for a small celebration."

"I'm going to have to take a rain check. I have some things I need to take care of this week. How about next weekend?"

"I have a date."

His brow furrowed. "Oh, I didn't know you were seeing anyone."

"It's relatively recent. Ivan asked to make me dinner next weekend."

"As in the warehouse guy?"

"Yes. He's not that bad, you have to admit."

He sighed. "You're right. You were right about him since the beginning, and we should have listened." Marco got up from his computer chair, throwing on his suit jacket that was laid over the headrest. "Congrats on your new gig, by the way. It's going to be fun working with another Dane."

I cocked my head and asked, "Why do I get the feeling you don't really mean that?"

"I'm not joking. I like working with your brother, and I'm sure I'll like working with you too."

I smiled. "I'm looking forward to many more cases with

you."

"I have to run, but I'm sure we'll be seeing a lot more of each other. Maybe we'll all be able to have that dinner together sometime soon."

"I'll hold you to it."

Marco gave me a half-smile before turning on his heel to leave the bullpen. I started to walk toward my new office, but I noticed a corner of the paper Marco had been looking at was sticking out of the drawer. I glanced over my shoulder, making sure he was gone before pulling the drawer open. I placed my box down on his unoccupied seat before picking up the letter. I knew I shouldn't have been digging into his personal life, but I was curious about what he was hiding.

Opening up the plain-white printer paper, the first thing to catch my attention was the polaroid picture. It was a close-up shot of a hand. It appeared to be a woman's hand, and it was severed from the body. On the back of the hand, there looked to be a brand seared into the skin. It was hard to make out, but as far as I could tell, it was a circle with three dots inside of it— two on top and one below. It almost looked like a low-graphic bowling ball, but I was sure it was something else entirely and had a deeper meaning to the person who'd used it. Part of me felt like I'd seen it before, yet I couldn't put a finger on where or how.

On the bottom section of the polaroid, a year was written in blue ink: *1997*. My eyes peered up to the main letter. There was only one sentence written out with very messy penmanship. It took over almost half the page and read: *DO YOU REMEMBER THIS DAY?*

The ominous note wasn't even directed toward me, but it sent a cold shiver down my spine. I wondered how Marco was involved in whatever event this may have been referencing. But judging by the look on his face when I had found him, he knew exactly what this mystery writer was talking about.

179

Thank you for Reading!

Dear Reader, I hope you've enjoyed reading *Sketching Undercover.* If you have the time, it would be greatly appreciated if you could leave a short review for the book. It doesn't just help the author, but future readers as well, and I'm sure they'd be thankful for it too.
Thank you!

Stay in Touch with T.K. Price

Follow T.K. Price on Facebook and Instagram:
Facebook: www.facebook.com/TKPriceauthor
Instagram: @t.k.price_Author
Website: https://tprice2author.wixsite.com/tpricethriller

I sincerely hope you enjoyed reading this book as much as I enjoyed writing it.

About the Author

T.K. Price doesn't actually exist. She's just a pen name for an author who does. Even if she's not necessarily real, the person she embodies likes to think she is, at least somewhat. T.K. Price is the half who loves a good mystery. Whether it's a light-hearted cozy mystery or a gritty crime fiction novel (or show), she is interested.

After many years of watching crime shows, playing Nancy Drew games, and reading mystery novels, T.K. Price decided to dive into the writing world herself and create her own beloved characters and scenarios. Her debut crime fiction novel, Sketching Undercover, is her first attempt to enter the mystery world. And her cozy mystery novel will soon follow.

T.K. Price lives in the sunny state of Florida with her family and fifteen-year-old Pomeranian.